W9-AAL-534

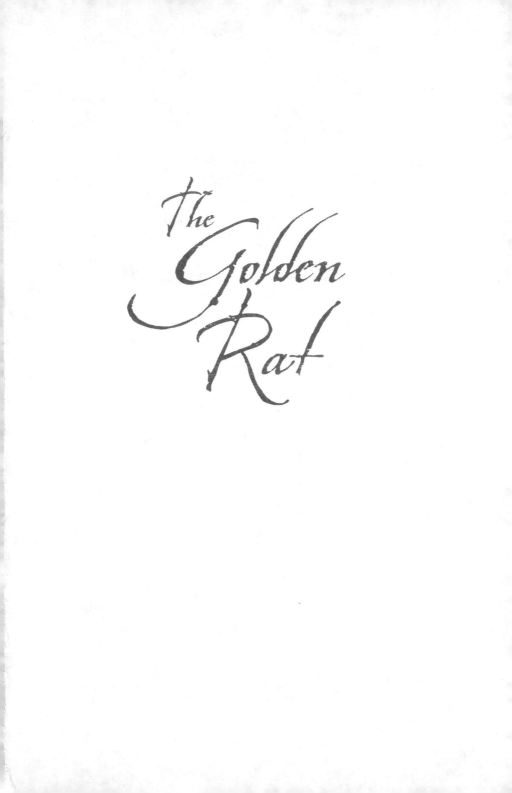

The Golden Rat

The Golden Rat

DON WULFFSON

BLOOMSBURY
CHILDREN'S
BOOKS

Published by Bloomsbury U.S.A. Children's Books
175 Fifth Avenue, New York, NY 10010
Distributed to the trade by Holtzbrinck Publishers

Library of Congress Cataloging-in-Publication Data
Wulffson, Don L.
The Golden Rat / by Don Wulffson.—1st U.S. ed.
p. cm.
Summary: When sixteen-year-old Baoliu is wrongfully accused of murdering his
stepmother, his father pays someone else to die in his place, leaving Baoliu to fend
for himself on the streets of twelfth-century China.
ISBN-13: 978-1-59990-000-1 • ISBN-10: 1-59990-000-9
1. China—History—960–1644—Juvenile fiction.
[1. China—History—960–1644—Fiction. 2. Mystery and detective stories.] I. Title.
PZ7.W96373Go 2007   [Fic]—dc22   2006032266

First U.S. Edition 2007
Typeset by Westchester Book Composition
Printed in the U.S.A. by Quebecor World Fairfield
2 4 6 8 10 9 7 5 3 1

All papers used by Bloomsbury U.S.A. are natural, recyclable products
made from wood grown in well-managed forests. The manufacturing processes
conform to the environmental regulations of the country of origin.

FOR JILL

1

BAOLIU FOUGHT TO keep his sanity, to somehow escape the horror. He walked in leg shackles; he paced from one end of the bamboo cage to the other, the chains connecting his ankles rattling, measuring out each step.

There were two others in the waiting cell. In one corner, a bony-looking boy rocked back and forth, beating the back of his head against the bamboo wall. He seemed about Baoliu's age, sixteen, but was small and runtlike, almost deformed. Nearby, an old man sat quietly, his chest a sagging display of tattoos. Baoliu felt the man's eyes following him. Their gazes met.

"Lengjing xia lai." "Calm yourself," he said, and then

patted Baoliu on the arm. "It will be over soon. Take what comfort you can in that." Baoliu looked at him blankly and turned away. An overpowering fear swept through him. His hands closed around thick, smooth bars; he pressed his face against them, and looked out— beyond the guardhouse to the execution yard. At dawn, he would be taken there and beheaded. Sick with dread, he stared at the place where he would die.

A MURDERER IS what Baoliu was in the eyes of the people of Yongjia. A bloody little thief and killer. But in reality perhaps his only sins had been to offend and disappoint his father.

The day before the crime had been even more unpleasant than usual. At the afternoon meal, waiting for it to be served, Baoliu's father began reminiscing. "As a child, I lived in Henan for a year. I worked in the rice fields there. Have I ever told you about it?"

"I don't think so," said Hai Nan, Baoliu's older brother. Baoliu shook his head—lying, like his brother. The story was one that they'd both heard countless times before.

"Every morning," said their father, "a drum was beaten to call the workers together. And then the drum was beaten all day long. The faster the beat, the faster we had to work."

Like the drumbeat he described, Baoliu's father went on and on, without stopping. Baoliu's mind began to wander. He tried to picture Henan, and the ancient monasteries and fortresses said to be found there. He thought of great adventures—of travels to far-off parts of China, and of battling the Mongol invaders of the North Country; he imagined himself in the jungles to the south, in the Viet territories, and in the vast deserts of Far Western China. And in his mind he pictured a girl he was fond of, Tao-an, and remembered something she had said to him once, something funny. He smiled to himself.

"Do my words bore you, Baoliu?"

He looked across the table. "No, of course not, Father," he said with false zeal. "I apologize."

Stroking his beard, for a long moment, his father gazed at him and then scowled and turned his attention to Hai Nan, and to business matters—to the making and selling of shoes. The family business, Footwear by Tang Qin & Sons, had flourished as the family had withered. How to increase productivity, how to increase profit—for them, it seemed to Baoliu, that is all there was anymore. Finding the least expensive leather, finding new markets, keeping costs to a minimum—no other subjects seemed of interest to them. They hunched forward like two conspirators, speaking across the low table, their heads almost touching, then paused for a moment, waiting as servants quietly served the meal.

Baoliu inhaled the pungent aroma of black tea, noodles, dumplings, and soy sauce. Through a blur of steam, his father and Hai Nan began eating and resumed their private dialogue. Only a token glance Baoliu's way from time to time indicated they even knew he was there.

He picked at his food, gazing beyond the dining area to the veranda and back gardens, and for a moment saw a vision of his mother tending the flowers there. She was wearing her favorite sun hat, quietly and contentedly going about her work.

The image vanished.

When his mother had died, only a year earlier, everything had changed. His father had become angry and bitter, and had begun to withdraw into his work. Hai Nan, his only brother, had turned into a stranger. Three years older than Baoliu, he was the first son and heir to the family business. Hai Nan had risen to the role of his father's confidante and partner. As he did, Baoliu's position had declined; as the second son, he had become no more than a valued assistant, and even in that lowly role had quickly become more of a burden than an asset: he was so often at odds with his father that he did his work indifferently and poorly.

And it was clear that Hai Nan would become the scholar of the family—its rising star. Already, he had passed the required examinations for admissions to the university in Hangzhou, and within the year would begin his studies of philosophy and literature. Baoliu dreaded the thought of shutting himself off from the world and devoting ten hours a day to study.

With each passing day, his father's respect for him had diminished—as had his for his father.

His father expected complete obedience and unquestioning acceptance of his wishes. In the past, Baoliu had always given him both; now he offered him neither.

To Baoliu's disgust, only four months after his mother's death, his father had taken a new wife—Tang Jia Lam, a beautiful, dull-witted woman half his age. He doted on her, gave her anything she wanted. A twittering fool.

Baoliu could hear her in the kitchen now, berating their cook, Lao Yu, and hear him kowtowing to her, mumbling timid apologies.

"Is the food not to your liking, Baoliu?"

He raised his gaze to meet his father's. "I'm enjoying it greatly," said Baoliu, and glanced down at his untouched meal. "Almost as much as the conversation. I only wish I had something to contribute. Forgive me if I've distracted you by not saying anything."

"Your sarcasm is not appreciated!"

"I didn't think it would be."

His father's dark eyes blazed, and he slapped the edge

of the table, making the plates jump. "You will kindly leave the room!"

"As you wish," said Baoliu, rising and then bowing stiffly.

"*Likai!*" "Go!"

Baoliu left the table and made his way upstairs to where an open balcony joined the wings of the estate. He pushed his long hair from his eyes. He took a deep breath and then exhaled noisily, gazing out upon the Tiantang district, at the sweet-smelling woods and the large collection of estates nestled amid the greenery. Through the trees he could see the city, and in the far distance stretched the Great Eastern Sea, reaching, it seemed, to the ends of the earth.

From downstairs, he could still hear Hai Nan and his father. They were talking about him.

"He's so contemptuous it makes me ill," he heard his father say. "I would never have believed a son of mine could act like he does."

"He's just young and immature," replied Hai Nan, defending Baoliu and insulting him in the same breath. "In time, I think he'll come around."

"*Ni Hao, qin ai qizi!*" "Hello, dear man!" Tang Jia Lam's grating voice joined his father's and brother's.

Baoliu glanced over the railing. And then stood listening to the nattering fool going on and on about nothing—and his father sounding as though it were all of great interest to him.

Jia Lam. She'd all but destroyed the family. Before she'd come into their lives, there had rarely been a harsh word between Baoliu and his father. Once, they had been like best friends. Now they fought constantly.

"It is not your place to judge me!" his father had told Baoliu a hundred times. And perhaps he was right. And perhaps he was right that Baoliu had become, as he put it, "shamefully disrespectful." Still, having the woman in the house was more than Baoliu could bear. Seeing his father dote on her—and seeing her take on his mother's role—revolted Baoliu.

The banter from the dining room dissolved into a clattering of dishware as the table was cleared. He heard his father return to his sleeping chamber only to reemerge minutes later at the front of the house. Gripping bamboo runners, porters lowered a sedan chair for him, and he stepped on the back of a servant and into the covered litter.

Somehow it was sad, watching him go, being trotted off to the city. Once he would have walked. Once he had been young, an artisan—a shoemaker, who had lived in crowded disarray with his family above a tiny shop in Yongjia. Once he had been happy.

But now he was a rich man, and old, the joy of ambition behind him.

Baoliu watched the other traffic on the roadway with indifference—until he realized a covered palanquin had stopped at their doorway. His fat, baldheaded tutor

Yinpao emerged, and leaning on a servant boy, rapped his cane on the door.

Baoliu listened as a servant greeted him, and then Hai Nan joined in. Creeping down the stairs, Baoliu watched as his brother and the rotund little man bowed to each other—warmly, as would a former pupil and teacher. They asked the expected and polite questions of the other, and then turned to the matter at hand.

"I must speak to your father about Baoliu," said Yinpao.

Baoliu continued down the stairs, and then stopped halfway as his tutor's gaze fell upon him.

"My father is not here," Baoliu told Yinpao.

Yinpao looked to Hai Nan and asked if this was so, and crossed fat arms into wide sleeves. "It is my unfortunate duty," he told Hai Nan, "to inform you that I have found Baoliu to be an unsatisfactory pupil. He has learned nothing, seems to have no interest in furthering his education, and is most discourteous. At our last session he argued with me. He interrupted me so frequently that I could no longer continue with the lesson. When I asked him the reason for his rudeness, he made no reply whatsoever, and simply got up and left. As you know, Hai Nan, I am a patient man; however, the situation has become too intolerable for me to even consider continuing as Baoliu's tutor. If you would kindly have your father visit me at his convenience, I will answer any questions he might have about the matter." From his purse, Yinpao produced several paper bills, hundred-tongqian notes, and pressed them into Hai Nan's hand. "Return this to your father, please—it is the tuition paid in advance for the remainder of the year."

Hai Nan nodded; he bade Yinpao farewell, and as he closed the door behind him, he turned to Baoliu. "So, another teacher washes his hands of you!" he exclaimed.

Baoliu shrugged. "Yinpao's an ass."

"Is he?" Hai Nan arched a brow.

"He bores me to death!"

"Really? When I had him as a tutor, I thought he was very interesting."

"*You* would!"

Hai Nan shook his head. He raised one finger and opened his mouth to speak.

" 'Interesting'?" Baoliu laughed, stopping Hai Nan before he could say anything. "How could you find that bag of wind interesting?"

"Perhaps if you listened you would learn something."

"It's the other way around. It was because I wasn't learning anything that I quit listening!"

"You interrupted him repeatedly at the last session—that is what he said. He is the teacher. You are the student. You're there to listen and learn, not argue."

"Even when he is wrong?"

"Ah, so you are smarter than he? More learned? Is that what you think?"

"No, certainly not. Yinpao has one of the finest minds in China. He has told me so himself!"

Shaking his head, Hai Nan turned to leave the room.

"Are you going to tell Father?" asked Baoliu, stopping him.

"Of course. What else would you have me do?"

"Just wait awhile to tell him—just a day or two."

"And what would *that* accomplish?"

"It might give me time—time before the two of them get together."

"You'd only be delaying the inevitable." Hai Nan stroked his sparse, almost invisible beard. "Yinpao expects me to inform Father, and that is what I am going to do. It's my responsibility, not only to him and Father, but also to you. It's time you began applying yourself."

"You sound just like Father! You talk like him. You think like him. You've even started to look like him!"

"Do I? Thank you for the compliment, Baoliu. It's most kind of you. And let me say that you would do well to be more like him yourself."

"I can't imagine anything worse!"

"You can't? Are you certain?"

"Quite," said Baoliu, and saw that Jia Lam, in a gown of pink-and-green brocade, was looking down from the second floor.

"*You shenne shi?*" "Is something amiss?" Smiling vacantly, she touched long fingernails to her painted face.

For a moment, her gaze lingered on Hai Nan. And then she cast a faint sneer in Baoliu's direction.

The gown—it had been his mother's, and the sight of it on Jia Lam sickened Baoliu. He tried to think of something clever to say, something that would embarrass her. Instead, he just scowled at her; he pushed past Hai Nan and then headed down the hall to his sleeping quarters. He kicked off his satin slippers. He stripped down to his undergarments, a loincloth and a long shirt, and then exchanged a silk robe for trousers and pulled on boots.

Hai Nan yelled something as he left the house.

"Zhukou, chunren!" "Shut up, fool!" he yelled back from the garden.

Insects buzzed. A crow squalled, and then flapped away.

Cursing under his breath, Baoliu ducked under a low branch and then made his way down a familiar path, one that wound through tall stands of bamboo and papyrus. He stopped and looked around to make sure that no one could see him, and then picked his way down a slope to where a misshapen cypress tree towered over dense undergrowth. Dropping to his knees, Baoliu crawled into a deep cleft in the trunk, and then, from its hiding place, lifted out an onyx box. He sat with it in his lap for a moment, and then opened it and removed his treasures: a little wooden bird his mother had carved for him when he was small, a pearl necklace, an ivory good-luck charm, and an opal ring set in gold. He slipped the ring on to the small finger of his left hand and began turning it, remembering when it had been on his mother's finger.

He remembered, too, when his father had given it to Jia Lam, and given her everything. Baoliu had asked his father for just a few of his mother's things to remember her by. Except for the hand-carved bird, his father had said no; Baoliu had sneaked into Jia Lam's private bedroom and taken the things anyway. His father had demanded that he return them, but all his shouting hadn't gotten him anywhere, and neither had half a dozen whippings. Baoliu refused to tell him where he'd hidden the pieces.

He replaced the box in its hiding place, and then he began hiking the trails beyond his house, moving fast and trying not to think too much. The air began to cool and the day faded, but he continued on, afraid of returning home, afraid of facing his father. He walked until his breath turned to puffs of gray and until there was nowhere to go and nothing to do but to turn and head back.

It had long since turned dark and cold by the time he finally returned to the house. Baoliu heard his brother's voice coming from an upstairs room. He heard the sound of Jia Lam laughing, and he smelled the rich scent of food lingering in the air. He peered into the dining area and found it empty; only a few dirty bowls and plates remained. He gulped tea from a half-empty cup and stuffed his mouth with leftover strips of spiced duck and pork.

Startling Baoliu, their cook, Lao Yu, emerged from the kitchen.

The little man quickly hid his surprise at finding Baoliu gobbling leftover food. He lowered his eyes, waiting for him to finish.

Embarrassed, Baoliu grabbed a plum and hurried off to his bedroom. He lit a candle in a lantern, lay back on his canopied bed, and took a bite of the fruit. He realized his father was standing in the doorway, looking in at him. Baoliu sat up, waiting for the tirade to begin.

"I spoke with your tutor this afternoon," he said simply. "Nothing he had to say about you was a surprise. Perhaps that is the saddest thing of all."

Baoliu tried to think of a response.

It was unnecessary; his father had left, and become a shadow disappearing down the hallway.

BAOLIU LISTENED AS the house was closed up for the night. He heard some servants chattering in the kitchen and others heading upstairs. A door closed.

He heard mounted constables pass by outside, and then mixed laughter from a nearby estate, one where a gathering of some kind was in its final throes.

He pulled off his boots and lay back on his bed, and kept seeing his father and hearing his words: *"Nothing he had to say about you was a surprise. Perhaps that is the saddest thing of all."* He stared at the ceiling, sick inside, angry at himself, angry at everybody. He thought about his father and Jia Lam, and Hai Nan and Yinpao. He thought about everything until his head ached.

He got to his feet. Still hungry, he made his way through the dark house to the kitchen. The larder, as he had expected, was locked for the night. He smelled the scent of pork rinds drying in the still-warm oven. He ate hungrily, and reached for more—and felt his sleeve catch on the stove. He grabbed frantically as a pot fell and bounced, banging across the floor.

"*Shenme shenyin?*" "What?" The voice was muffled, coming from upstairs.

Baoliu hurried from the kitchen—and then froze, as a disembodied lantern seemed to float down the stairs.

"*Shi shei?*" "Who's there?" His father's voice was hard, anxious.

Baoliu backed away, looking for a place to hide, as the lantern was raised, enveloping him in wavering light.

"Baoliu!"

"I'm sorry." Baoliu stepped into the open, toward his father's amber-lit face. "I was trying to be quiet," he mumbled. "I knocked something over."

"What are you doing prowling around like this?"

Baoliu heard a door open above and then saw Jia Lam peering out from her private quarters.

"I was hungry. I just wanted something to eat," said Baoliu.

"Go to bed!"

Baoliu looked at his father, and at a maid peering around the corner, and, without a word, made his way back to his room.

"And stay there!" his father shouted after him.

BAOLIU AWOKE SUDDENLY, thinking he had heard something. He had fallen asleep in his clothes, and wondered why.

The sound came again—footsteps; he looked up as someone passed in the hallway—a servant, perhaps.

Baoliu thought nothing of it, and pulled covers around himself, but then his eyes came to rest on the lantern next to his bed. The candle had almost burned itself out and now flickered faintly in a puddle of wax. He felt as though he'd only drifted off for a few minutes, but in fact, he'd been asleep for hours. It was late, probably near dawn. Why would anyone be up so early?

Yawning, he crawled out of bed. He looked down the hallway, and saw a shadow headed up the stairs.

It must be Hai Nan, he thought for a moment, and then wasn't sure.

He pulled on a robe and slippers and crept into the main salon, picking his way through a dark maze of armchairs and tables, and then looked up the stairway. The shadowy figure was gone.

A door clicked open on the landing above.

Baoliu froze, and saw the shadow again, walking

through the dark on the landing. It pushed open a sleeping–chamber door—Jia Lam's—and then disappeared into her room.

"You shenme shi?" "What?" Her voice was faint, sleepy.

Baoliu couldn't make out the words, but it was a man who responded to her.

Something fell. And then quiet returned. Baoliu began to climb the stairs, slowly, quietly. And then froze as faint cries came from the room.

Immediately, Baoliu sprinted up the stairs and then across the landing. He was reaching for the half-open door; it suddenly swung outward, slamming into his face and knocking him reeling.

A scream came from inside the room.

Someone stumbled over Baoliu, fingernails digging into his neck. He turned, and the shadow of a foot smashed into his head.

He rolled onto his stomach, and felt hot blood dripping from his eyebrow. He tried to get to his knees, and crumpled face-first to the floor.

WAVES OF NAUSEA swept over him as he tried to awaken and open his eyes. He heard servants and heard his father crying out—and then it was later, it seemed, and he heard heavy boots and hard voices.

Hai Nan was explaining something, and then another voice joined in.

Baoliu blinked, blood in his eyes, and saw Hai Nan in his maroon robe. He saw men in hardened-leather armor—constables. And watched servants hurrying with basins in their hands.

"He's never liked her," said Hai Nan. "But *this* is unthinkable!" Jewelry was scattered on the floor. And a blanket was rolled up against the wall. The thing was mummy-shaped and bloody, and part of a hand was sticking out of the folds.

"Baoliu? What did you do?" his father cried, directly over him.

Baoliu struggled to get up, and realized his wrists were bound behind him. A gloved hand grabbed him by the shirt, and almost lifted him off his feet.

"What are you doing?" he cried.

"Zhukou!" "Silence!" the constable snapped.

"I did nothing!"

He was slammed against the wall. Dizzy, for a moment he saw his father looking on. And then he was being dragged down the stairs, held under the arms by two constables.

In front of the house, a crowd had gathered—neighbors, many still in their nightgowns.

A hum of voices stopped suddenly as Baoliu emerged in the grasp of the constables. Familiar eyes met his; people stepped back, and the crowd parted as he was led away.

3

TANG QIN COULD have let his son be taken to Yongjia Prison, a converted fortress about which tales of torture, death, and depravity abounded. Instead, at a cost of almost a hundred tongqian a day, Baoliu was confined in the Gaoji, the "jail of the rich," in a private cell within the walls of the House of Law, a collection of imposing buildings on a ridge overlooking the city.

The cell was small and sparse: a cot, a table, and a single, slitlike window, but it was clean, he was given three meals a day, and his other needs were tended to. Still, though he was well treated and ate passable food, Baoliu didn't consider himself the least bit fortunate.

He'd done nothing. He'd committed no crime; his father or Hai Nan or one of the servants had killed Jia Lam. One of them had stabbed her to death. Or maybe it had been done by an intruder, a thief. Whoever it had been, it was Baoliu alone who would have to answer for the crime.

He was told there would be a trial, but not when it might be.

Prisoners in Gaoji were allowed to receive food, clothing, and other things from relatives, and to have visitors. Baoliu kept waiting for someone to come see him, or at least send a package. No packages arrived and no visitors came, not even his father or brother.

Day after day, he languished—terrified of the impending trial, outraged by what had happened to him. *How could father do this to me?* he wondered over and over. *How could he turn his back on me, abandon me like this? How could he think I'd ever kill someone?*

On the morning of his fourth day in the prison, the numbing anxiety of waiting turned to sick fear. The guards came for him; in shackles, he was escorted through the House of Law and into a large, wood-paneled courtroom—the place musty, stinking of a stale odor and age. He saw his father and Hai Nan, and some of his relatives, but most of the seats were empty. Not one of his friends was there. There was a clerk in a black skullcap, and a black-robed judge hunched over an ornately carved table, a writing brush in one hand, the other resting on an ivory cudgel. His face was long and thin, his mouth pinched-looking.

Shackled, wearing the same bloodied clothes he'd had on the night of the murder, Baoliu stood before him, guards at his side. The judge looked up from his writing and studied Baoliu. "I have examined the magistrate's report, and it is his conclusion that you are guilty of the crime of murder. Your confession is now required."

"I killed no one," said Baoliu, his voice cracking with nerves. "I do not confess."

The judge blinked. "Very well. Then you shall proceed to speak in your defense and to present evidence of your innocence. Defend yourself if you can."

"I have never killed anyone, and I never would. I did not kill Jia Lam."

"Then who did?"

"I don't know," said Baoliu, and glanced over his shoulder at the people behind him. "I saw someone go into her room, but I don't know who it was."

"And why don't you know?"

"It was close to dawn but still very dark."

The judge leaned back in his chair. "And you just happened to be awake at this time?"

"I was asleep, but then something woke me up—footsteps, or some other sound."

"'Or some other sound,'" said the judge, softly echoing Baoliu's words.

Baoliu licked his dry lips. "When I heard her cry, I ran to help."

"You rushed to her rescue?"

"Yes."

"How brave of you!" said the judge, a smile veiling his sarcasm.

"It's the truth!"

Someone laughed, a stupid, jittery giggle coming from somewhere behind Baoliu. The judge pounded for quiet. He smiled into the silence he had created and then turned his gaze on Baoliu.

"Perhaps I am mistaken," he said in a pleasant, mild-sounding tone of voice, "but there are stains on your clothing which appear to be dried blood."

"It's *my* blood." With a shackled hand, Baoliu touched the gash in his forehead. "The bedroom door hit me and I bled. The rest of it must have gotten on me when the killer stumbled into me when he was trying to get away."

"Oh, I see," said the judge, as though suddenly enlightened and fully believing Baoliu's every word.

Baoliu opened his mouth to speak.

"This 'killer'? No one else in your family saw him. Why were you the only one?"

"The others were asleep."

"But didn't you say that Jia Lam cried out? Wouldn't this have awakened everybody?"

"Yes—I think it did."

"But still no one saw him?"

"No, but—"

"There's something else I don't understand," interrupted the judge, his tone one of mock confusion. "You claim to have been asleep in bed and awakened by a noise. However, when the constables found you, you were fully dressed. Why?"

Baoliu's words wavered with nerves. "The night before the robbery, I returned home late. I was tired—and fell asleep in my clothes."

"Oh," said the judge as the clerk handed him a document. He studied it for a long moment and then looked up at Baoliu. "Jewelry was stolen that night, some of which has not been found, and I see here that you have stolen from your father's wife before. Is this so?"

"Yes," said Baoliu, rubbing damp palms on his pants. "But I wasn't stealing from Jia Lam that night."

"Oh, this night was an exception?" The judge laughed softly at his own joke, and then so did the clerk and the guards.

"The things I took before were things that had been my mother's. When my mother died, Jia Lam took everything that had belonged to her. I couldn't let her keep all of it."

"Is this correct: Jia Lam became your father's wife after the death of your mother? How did you feel about her? Did you like Jia Lam?"

"No."

"Did you resent her?"

"Yes, I did, but—"

"Did you hate her?"

Baoliu tried to think of something to say but no words would come.

His gaze on Baoliu, the judge sighed and then looked out at the courtroom. "Does anyone wish to speak in defense of Baoliu?" he asked. "Are any present who can attest to his innocence?"

Baoliu turned and looked at his father and brother and the others, and tears filled his eyes; none of them moved, none of them rose to address the court.

"I find no reason, then," said the judge, "not to confirm the conclusion of the magistrate. I declare you guilty of the crime of murder."

Baoliu stared openmouthed.

"Your age of only sixteen years inclines me to leniency. Though your crime was most heinous, a capital punishment can be avoided. With your confession, a sentence of enslavement for life will be the recommendation of this court. How do you say?"

"I did nothing wrong!"

"Baoliu, it is most evident that you *did!*" said the judge, his voice rising. "I think you now regret what you have done—but only because of the price you will have to pay, not because you are repentant. Think of all the pain and grief you have caused. Show contrition for what you have done, admit to your wrongdoing, and you may be spared."

"Confess, Baoliu!" Hai Nan called out. "Save yourself!"

"I confess to nothing!"

"Then no choice remains for me!" snapped the judge. "Death by beheading is the sentence of this court!"

"I'm not guilty! I murdered no one!"

Rising darkly, the judge aimed the cudgel at him. "Guards! Remove him!"

"Just time!" he begged. "Just give me time to prove my innocence!" Baoliu reached out chained hands.

A huge arm locked around his neck; another guard grabbed the loop of chain connecting his wrist shackles. Hai Nan cried out to him and his father hung his head in shame as Baoliu was dragged from the courtroom.

4

BEFORE THE TRIAL, Baoliu had held out hope. Now he had none.

Now, like the other two in the waiting cell, he sat—thinking over and over about everything that had happened—and about what was to come. The under-sized boy had quit beating his head back against the bars, and now sat staring into space; the tattooed old man lay curled in sleep.

Baoliu pressed his face against thick, dirty bars and gazed emptily out at the prison complex.

Guards paced the ramparts of the prison-yard walls.

A work gang was collecting its tools and taking them to a shed. They'd worked most of the day refurbishing a barrier between the execution yard and the spectator's gallery. The job appeared done; everything was ready for the morning show.

The afternoon waned. The gold of day changed to darkening silver as the sun dipped beneath distant hills, striping the cell and those inside with lengthening shadows of bamboo. His feet caked with mud, his silk robe and cotton shirt and pants filthy, Baoliu hugged himself against the cold.

Far below, the Oujiang River slowly snaked through the plains, black and sluggish-looking, melding opaquely with a fog-draped sea. From the heart of the city, the *Genggu*, The Drum of Time, began to beat, announcing the first of the twelve hours of the night.

Darkness closed in on the cage. Baoliu hung his head, wishing for the morning. He only wanted it to be over— for the pain of waiting to end. He had seen death before, but believed that somehow it did not apply to him. He was going to live forever.

Muffled laughter erupted from the guardhouse.

If only I'd confessed, he kept telling himself. *My life would have been spared.* Anything was better than death.

More laughter came from the guardhouse.

Baoliu looked in the direction of the place.

A door squealed open. A torch seemed to be floating

in the direction of the bamboo death cell. Footsteps crackled. Two guards, one with a torch in hand, emerged into view.

Bathed in wavering light, Baoliu exchanged glances with the boy and old man.

Fingers fumbled with a lock. The cage door swung open.

"Tang Baoliu! To your feet!"

Baoliu found himself facing a gap-toothed guard. Chewing a wad of sap, the man closed iron cuffs on Baoliu's wrists as the other removed his leg shackles.

"Come!" He was pulled out into flickering light. He looked all around, at the black outline of the main prison and the towering walls encircling it, and then at the execution yard and the spectators' gallery there. *Run!* His own voice screamed inside his head.

"*Kuai yidian!*" "Move!" ordered the sap-chewing guard. And then he jabbed Baoliu in the back, pushing him in the direction of the guardhouse.

"Where are you taking me?" A curse was his answer—and the sting of a split-cane whip across his back. He stumbled ahead, sharp stones digging into his feet, and then was shoved ahead into a long, paved corridor. Yellow light streamed from the last doorway. He followed it into a small room.

"Father!"

Tang Qin sat at a scratched wooden table—alone, his expression hard, his eyes tired. For a long moment he looked at Baoliu's shackled wrists and then slowly raised his gaze.

"*Zuoxia!*" A guard snapped his fingers and pointed in the direction of a low stool. "Sit!" he ordered.

Baoliu sat down across from his father, who averted his gaze. When he spoke it was as though he were addressing the wall beside him instead of his son.

"Arrangements have been made with the authorities. I have sacrificed a great deal of my money—eight thousand tongqian. It has cost me dearly, but your life is to be spared."

"What?" Baoliu gasped.

"There is to be a *ka-di*; another is to die in your place."

Shocked, Baoliu stared. He understood the arrangement his father had made—but not why. The custom, *ka-di*, was well known but its practice rare: at an enormous price, a substitute could be purchased to die in place of a criminal condemned by the courts.

Baoliu's eyes brimmed with tears. Relief—and gratitude—filled him. "Thank you, Father!" he stammered. "I know how all this must appear to you." He reached out a hand to his father, and then lowered it as his father, a look of contempt on his face, crossed his arms.

"Father, please, you've got to believe me when I tell you that I'm innocent!"

"*Zhukou!*" "Silence!" His fist came down hard on the table. "I am not your father, and never again shall you address me as such. After tonight, you shall not speak to me nor shall you ever again enter my home!"

Stunned, Baoliu clenched his jaw and wiped at tears brimming in his eyes. "I am innocent! I was not stealing from Jia Lam, and I did not kill her!"

"Even now you continue lying! And by lying, disgrace yourself even further!"

"I'm telling the truth!"

"You hated Jia Lam; you have since the first day she came into our home. You disrespected her, as you did me. You've fought with her; you've stolen from her; and now you've killed her! You say someone else was in the house that night, but I recall seeing only one person sneaking about in the dark that night—you!"

"You don't understand!"

"No, Baoliu, I do not. I do not understand what has happened to the son I once had! You lie, you steal, and now you've taken a life. You have committed the greatest of sins. You have dishonored this family for all time. Even now, you show no remorse for what you have done!"

"But I didn't do it!" Baoliu's hands curled into fists. "And somehow I'll prove it!"

His father exhaled noisily. "Do you think that I *want* to believe that a child of mine committed murder? Don't you realize how badly I want to believe you, and that I have tried to think of anything—*anything!*—that might make me even *doubt* that you're guilty? How I wish, with all my soul, that I could, but I can't!"

Baoliu opened his mouth to speak, and then stopped himself as a battered rosewood door opened. A magistrate in a red silk robe entered the room, followed by a guard and a man with a shaved head: Baoliu's substitute in death. His face looked oddly familiar and so did his hands. They were overlarge, the backs of them burned— scarred to a horrid, melted-looking smoothness. Their eyes met briefly and then the man was led from the room. The magistrate, stroking a beard of black and gray, turned to Baoliu. From the flowing sleeves of his robe he produced a scroll and read:

"Be it known that Tang Baoliu, son of Tang Qin, stands convicted of the crime of murder. By the gracious mercy of our emperor, the divine Ninzong, by arrangement of ka-di, he shall be allowed to live until such a time as he might, through misconduct or criminal endeavor, prove himself unworthy of this clemency; and revocation of these proceedings in this matter shall be undertaken." He looked down at Baoliu. "Do you understand these conditions?"

"Yes," Baoliu managed to say.

"Then you understand that any criminal act on your part shall result in retrial on a charge of murder."

He nodded woodenly.

Sick inside, Baoliu hung his head, and then looked up as the magistrate handed his father a writing brush and a bowl of red ink. For a long moment, Tang Qin gazed emptily at his son. He returned his attention to the document, signed it, and then, without a word, walked out of the room.

BAOLIU EXPECTED TO be set free immediately. Instead, the magistrate sat down across from him, and resting his chin on his hand, smiled.

"Tomorrow should prove to be a most interesting day for you," he said.

Baoliu said nothing, wondering what he meant.

"You shall see something that few of us experience in a lifetime."

"What?" Baoliu asked nervously.

The magistrate cocked his head. "You don't know?" he asked.

"No."

"Tomorrow you shall have the opportunity to see an innocent man executed for your crimes."

"What?"

"The peasant who is to die for you—you are to bear witness to his demise." He smiled, made his way to Baoliu, put a hand on his shoulder—and suddenly kicked the chair out from under him, sending him sprawling.

"Get him out of here," he told the guard. "You know what to do."

Stunned, wiping blood from the corner of his mouth, Baoliu was yanked to his feet and pulled through a side door into a passageway, torches in iron sconces lighting the way. Two more guards joined the first and Baoliu found himself following them out into the cool night air.

"Where are we going?"

One of them pointed toward the execution yard.

"Why?" cried Baoliu as another guard pushed him along toward an area of raised ground surrounded by high, fat lengths of sharpened bamboo.

" 'Why?' " mimicked a guard, a boy no older than Baoliu. " 'Why?' " he said again, and laughed, exposing toothless gums.

"Please!" Baoliu begged, starting to panic.

"*Niguixia!*" "Kneel!" snarled a skinny guard as they reached the yard.

He stared at the three. "Why? What are you going to do to me?"

" '*What are you going to do to me?*' " whined the toothless one.

Baoliu screamed. A club slammed into the back of his legs and dropped him to his knees. Panting, on all fours, he watched as his shackles were locked to a ringbolt in the ground.

"You didn't think it was over, did you?" A hand grabbed him by the hair and pulled his head back. "Rich little bastard," hissed the guard, his breath reeking of garlic. "Did you really think your father's money would save you?"

"Justice must be done!" exclaimed the skinny one, and drew a sword from its scabbard. And then touched the blade to the back of Baoliu's neck.

Baoliu turned to stone. He could not move—or speak—or think. In its shadow, he saw the sword raised high overhead. And then, with a will of its own, his head lowered and his eyes closed as he awaited the impact. But instead heard laughter and the receding shuffle of feet.

"The look on the little shit's face!" One of the guards chuckled. "Did you see?"

The bunch burst into inane howling.

Baoliu pushed himself to his feet. *"Baichi!"* "Idiots!" he shouted after them—only to go rigid with fear as they turned and headed back at him.

One with dead-black eyes came close. "What?" The man snarled, engulfing Baoliu in his fetid breath. "What did you say, boy?"

Baoliu stared wide-eyed. A fist slammed into his belly and then another came at him in a blur. After that, he remembered nothing.

HIS HEAD THROBBED, pounding him awake. He opened his eyes onto an overcast morning, and to walls of pointed bamboo. Still chained to the ringbolt in the ground, he sat up—wretched, filthy, his clothes damp with dew. He heard voices, and saw that a crowd had begun to form, in the spectator's gallery and on a grassy hill beyond.

A wheelbarrow filled with baskets and shovels rattled

past. From the steps of the guardhouse a soldier yelled across the yard. A servant trotted toward him.

Baoliu watched as the crowd grew, trying to ignore them, trying not to think about the butchery soon to come. He looked off beyond the enclosure to the main prison, where faces filled every window overlooking the execution yard.

"*Zaijian!*" "Good-bye!" A strange, high-pitched voice laughed .

Baoliu studied the windows, trying to spot the one from which the voice had come. He could not, even though the sick farewell continued to be repeated. He wondered which bothered him more—the taunting of the one or the silence of the rest.

A guard knelt in front of him and removed his leg shackles. Another pulled Baoliu to his feet and pushed him forward. Across the way, the magistrate, wearing a red silk robe and flanked by guards, wagged one finger, beckoning him. And at Baoliu's approach, pointed to a stool facing the onlookers.

"For your comfort," said the magistrate, smiling cruelly.

Mortified, Baoliu sat. A gallery of faces stared at him. He hung his head and looked away in shamed panic.

"Let them see you," cooed the magistrate.

Sharp fingernails dug into the back of his neck and then turned his head to face the crowd.

"Bear witness to Tang Baoliu!" the magistrate bellowed. "A *Jin Haozi*, a Golden Rat! A convicted murderer, he lives because another will die! Be it known that he is an outlaw and shall live henceforth outside the protection of legal authority. By people of good character he is to be shunned and forever despised, for he is at one now with the toad, the worm, and the cockroach—vermin of the most vile and repulsive nature! He is a creature without worth, without honor. He walks now in the footsteps of the dead, in those of an innocent man, and shall do so for all time!"

At first the crowd was silent, but then all at once, they began shouting and mocking Baoliu.

"You!" cried a girl from the grassy hill, her voice rising above the rest. Wearing a black shawl of mourning, she pointed at Baoliu. *"Youqian zhu!"* "Rich pig!"

He looked away—and his eyes came to rest on a gathering of familiar faces, those of neighbors from the Tiantang district. And then he recoiled in horror, for amid them were his father and brother.

"Jin Haozi!" "Golden Rat!" someone yelled.

Others joined in, the words becoming a chant.

"I did nothing!" Baoliu screamed at the crowd. "I am innocent!"

Laughter erupted.

"I am innocent!" he screamed again.

The crowd roared.

Baoliu hung his head, humiliated—wanting to hide. And then heard the crowd falling silent.

Over his shoulder he saw the tattooed old man and the boy being led into the execution yard. The man looked at Baoliu—and then, seeming to suddenly realize that there was to be a *ka-di*, leered at him with disgust, and then spat. The boy was too terrified to notice anything; he wrestled with his guards and squealed obscenities.

"Are you enjoying yourself?" The magistrate touched the back of Baoliu's neck.

Ice went down Baoliu's spine.

An excited hum rose from the crowd and every head turned as the executioner emerged from the guardhouse and quietly made his way into the execution yard. He did not seem particularly large or strong, and that was the most terrifying thing of all about the man—other than the yellow headband he wore as a symbol of his occupation, he looked quite ordinary. The magistrate began to pace from one prisoner to the next, looking each in the face. He stopped in front of the old man. And then, as one might do a friend, put a hand on his shoulder.

"It will be over soon. Take what comfort you can in that." Over and over, Baoliu kept hearing the old man's words as he watched him kneel and then slowly lower his head.

The executioner unsheathed his sword. He selected a spot behind the prisoner and set his legs in a broad stance. And then raised the sword high overhead.

Baoliu looked away. He didn't want to see—but looked back too soon, as the sword struck and the head tumbled. The crowd cheered; Baoliu's mouth opened in a silent scream.

The boy began to cry and then flail wildly as guards grabbed hold of him and forced him down. He kept writhing and trying to turn his head; it took three blows from the sword before the awful chore was done.

And then hooded eyes were looking into Baoliu's. "The best is yet to come." The magistrate smiled.

A profound quiet settled over everything. Baoliu watched as his substitute, a red sash of honor about his waist, unshackled and unguarded, entered the execution yard. He looked at Baoliu as he passed, and Baoliu wanted to scream: he remembered the man. He had been his father's employee.

On his own, the man knelt. His body trembled as he took two symbolic coins in his pink, burn-scarred hands.

"Behold Shen Manfong!" the magistrate bellowed at the crowd. "For eternity, speak of him with respect. Honor him, for he now gives his life for others! For his family! For the people of Yongjia! To each he gives equally, and pays with the currency of his very existence!"

"*Huzzah!*" shouted the crowd in a salute of respect. "*Huzzah!*"

The executioner was handed his sword.

Arms stretched wide, in each burn-scarred hand the

substitute clutched one of the coins. "Father!" the girl on the hillside wailed.

It's his daughter! Baoliu realized. His face rigid, the substitute gazed in her direction and then lowered his head. A moment later, the head lay in the dust. One eye was shut; the other was open—and seemed fixed on Baoliu.

"You are free to go," the magistrate hissed. Dark eyes, like those of a lizard, blinked slowly.

A guard removed Baoliu's shackles and then handed him a pair of satin slippers, the same ones he had been wearing on the night of the murder. He pulled them on as a platter-faced guard opened the gate.

"Golden Rat." He sneered.

Baoliu said nothing. Feeling oddly numb, he walked out of the gate—and suddenly found himself being pelted with garbage. A gob of spit hit him in the face. He wiped the slime off himself, retreating as a mob surged toward him and then engulfed him—punching at him, buffeting him from side to side. A fist glanced off his jaw, and someone grabbed him by his long hair and spun him around. He fell face-first; he crawled, struggled back to his feet.

"*Zhushou!*" "Stop!" he shouted, backing away from hate-filled faces.

A boy came at Baoliu, only to be stopped by a guard; and then more guards stepped in front of the crowd.

Baoliu backpedaled and then turned and ran.

A stone grazed the side of his face; he stumbled, as more sailed past, and then slid down an embankment and kept running. The way ahead narrowed, and then closed in on him as he entered a stretch of marshland.

Panting, his feet sinking in muck and water, he pushed his way through wet brambles. He crawled over a fallen tree and then found himself on a patch of dry ground. Looking back through dead branches, he saw no one. Exhausted, he dropped to his knees; his shoulders began to heave, and he put a hand to his face and began to sob.

5

BAOLIU WIPED GARBAGE off his clothes and ran his fingers through his hair, brushing out more of it. He swept aside leaves from the surface of a pool of stagnant water, then submerged his hands. He scrubbed them together; he cupped them and washed the worst of the blood and dirt off his face and arms.

He itched all over, and everything hurt.

Rubbed raw by shackles, his wrists and ankles burned, and pain shot through his left shoulder from the fall he'd taken. His face was scratched, his jaw ached, and he kept running his tongue over a cut inside his cheek. He put a hand to his forehead and felt at the scabbed-over gash there, dried blood flaking away at the touch.

The murder. The trial. The executions. All of it kept coming back at Baoliu.

Who had killed Jia Lam? Who had he seen going up the stairs that night?

And then there was the substitute, Shen Manfong, a man whose name he didn't remember until the day of the executions. He had once worked for Baoliu's father, first as a shoemaker and later as a tanner. But then he'd scalded his hands and been unable to continue working, and Baoliu had seen little of him—until the night the agreement was signed.

Why had the man offered his life in *ka-di*? What had happened to make him desperate enough to want to do such a thing?

Probably, Baoliu would never know, and perhaps it really didn't matter. For now, all that mattered was surviving.

But where would he go? To whom could he turn? Not one of his friends had come to his trial, nor had many of his relatives. And no one had risen in his defense when it had come time to speak.

He would not go begging at their doors, any more than he would at his father's. He would take care of himself. He'd find work, do whatever was necessary to get by.

Baoliu undid the single braid into which his hair had been tied, and let it fall to his shoulders. Then he took the sash from his silk robe and tied it on as a headband. He took off the robe and tossed it into the bushes, and then tried to think of some other way to alter his appearance. The satin slippers he wore, though sodden and caked with mud, were those of a rich boy. He kicked them off. Looking at them lying in dirty water, he tried to remember when his father had given them to him.

Barefoot, wearing only cotton pants and an undershirt, he pushed his way into the marsh again. In rank water up to his ankles, he picked his way past tangles of fallen branches and heaps of rotting foliage. The water rose to his knees and then almost to his waist before the soft muck underfoot began to ascend and then finally turn to solid ground. From somewhere ahead he could hear the sound of people and traffic.

Pushing tall grass aside, he found himself emerging onto a backstreet of Yongjia.

In the distance he could see a place he knew all too well, the family business, Tang Qin & Sons, a large, green-painted shop where some of the finest footwear in Yongjia had once been crafted. Now, only sandals were made, for the military, for its foot soldiers. The cost was low, the demand never-ending, and the profit great.

For as long as Baoliu could remember, the shop had been part of his life. He had played there as a child—usually pretending to be a shoemaker. As he grew, he learned the trade. Few days had passed without him helping out in some way or another.

But now he had no wish to go near the place.

He made a detour.

The route was an unfamiliar one, down through a wretched marketplace, the air foul, ripe with the stench of food and trash of every sort. Beggars held out empty bowls. Peddlers hawked their wares from pushcarts and stalls. Carpeting, clothing, and tools—every type of merchandise was offered for sale or barter. In butcher shops, cuts of meat, swarming with flies, hung from rafters, as did live chickens, their squawking punctuating the noisy drone of voices and other sounds.

He felt as though every eye were on him; he glanced at faces as he walked, and saw only indifference, people caught up in their own lives, unaware of him, uninterested.

From ahead on the narrow street came a loud crunch, and then a yell and curses, as the roadway quickly became clogged with traffic. The wheel of an oxcart had shattered, and melons and squash were tumbling down as the driver screamed at people to get away.

A little girl snatched up a fast-rolling melon and darted off. And then others were grabbing for the rest.

"Xiaotou!" "Thieves!" screamed the driver.

"Bikai!" "Out of the way!"

Across the street, two constables in hardened-leather armor bullied their way toward the scene.

Baoliu backed away. Getting free of the logjam, he made his way into an open-air market, one where flowers were sold—and almost walked into a girl he knew, Si An, the daughter of family friends.

"Baoqian!" "Excuse me!" she said, and began to bow, but then recognition showed in her eyes. The beginning of a smile stopped.

"Don't worry, Si An, I'm not going to kill you," he wanted to say. Instead, he just frowned at her and left.

Across the way was a cobbler's shop. He asked about work. A young woman looked him up and down—at his dirty, bloodstained clothes. She waved him away, a look of disgust on her face. He tried two more shops, both with the same result.

He made his way through an alley and then down into the town square. Everywhere, there were food stands and carts, piled high with fruits, vegetables, and sweet rolls. He looked longingly at them, and at vendors selling sweet tea and fruit juices from vases strapped to their backs. He licked his lips, swallowed, watched a woman at a stand where snakes were being sold. Some were still alive. Others had already been skinned and transformed into long loops of meat. Chunks of it, skewered with pieces of onion and green pepper, sizzled on a charcoal brazier.

Stonemasons were digging up paving stones and re-setting them; Baoliu sidestepped the men and found a place in a narrow strip of shade beneath the flaring eaves of a restaurant. He wiped sweat from his face and rubbed his sore shoulder.

A boy knelt down beside Baoliu. His clothes were

ragged; a bundle made from an old blanket was strapped to his back; his head was shaved. Twisted around, he was trying to reach behind himself, to the back of his foot where a dark splinter was stuck in his heel. He picked at it awkwardly, without result, seeming unable even to see it clearly.

"Can I help?" Baoliu asked.

He looked Baoliu up and down. "Yeah, thanks," he said, his expression hard, unreadable.

The foot was rough, thickly callused, the splinter angled up under the skin behind the heel. Baoliu tried again and again to get hold of the thing.

The boy slipped a knife from its sheath and handed it to him. "Use that," he said.

Baoliu cut a nick in the skin. The boy did not so much as wince; he just looked over his shoulder. Baoliu pressed the blade under the tiny shaft and pinched it between a fingernail and the knife. Then pulled it free.

"Thanks," he said.

"My pleasure."

The boy pulled a brown gourd from its shoulder strap, then poured water onto the back of his heel. He took a swallow from its wooden spigot and then handed it to Baoliu.

Water had never tasted so good.

"That's him, I tell you! It's Baoliu!"

Baoliu tensed; he looked around, not sure where the voice had come from.

"Get him!" At first he saw only the milling crowd. But then three boys came into view, and then a fourth emerged from the downstairs of a multistory wood building.

"*Haozi!*" yelled Chen Mingna, the only one of the bunch he recognized. This boy and his father had once worked as gardeners for Baoliu's family. He had never spoken to Baoliu, but there was always contempt in his eyes and the edge of a smile on his lips. Now it was a broad, cruel grin.

"What do you want?"

"I saw the executions this morning." The boy smirked. "And I saw you sitting there like the rich little ass you are, sitting there on that stool. You looked so scared!" He chuckled, exchanged glances with his friends. "Why were you so scared, Baoliu?"

Baoliu said nothing. Kneeling, wiping blood from his heel, the boy he had helped looked up at him quizzically—and then at Chen Mingna.

"What were you so afraid of? It wasn't *your* head that was going to be chopped off. It wasn't as though they were going to execute *you* for killing your father's new little wife. Someone else had to die for it, not you!"

A small crowd had begun to form.

"What do you want from me?"

The four moved closer, fanned out. Chen Mingna laughed, and began beating his fist against his open palm.

Baoliu realized the ragged boy was standing at his side. "Can I help?" he asked, smiling wryly.

"Who are you?" Chen Mingna scowled.

"Just a friend," he said.

"Stay out of it, peasant boy!" he hissed, aiming a finger and then jabbing the ragged boy in the chest.

"Don't do that again."

Chen Mingna grinned, pushed him—and an instant later lay facedown on the pavement, gagging and gasping for breath: all in one motion, the boy had grabbed Chen Mingna's wrist, pulled him forward, and driven an open hand deep into his stomach.

Two others came forward. Baoliu launched himself at them, and ended up in a flailing heap, rolling over and over with them. A fist slammed into Baoliu's mouth. He spat blood, then found himself wrestling with one of them, punching at his head.

Somewhere, hooves clattered loudly; the crowd parted as constables on horseback descended on the brawl. The horses wheeled, rose up on hind legs, as their riders slapped and slashed at the bunch with bamboo whips.

"Goule!" "Enough!" shouted one of the constables.

Blows continued raining down on the boys, pounding them apart. Baoliu grabbed the arm of the boy who'd come to his aid and pulled him to his feet. They ran.

They raced down a long alleyway. They'd almost reached the end of it when Baoliu heard thundering hooves, and glancing over his shoulder caught a glimpse of two constables.

"Here they come!" he yelled.

People turned and watched them. Chickens squawked and jumped out of their way. They slapped through clothes hung out to dry and turned a corner, into a crowded street.

"Don't run." The boy panted, grabbing Baoliu's arm. "And don't look back. If you do, they'll spot us."

They walked, struggling to catch their breath, losing themselves in the crowd. Baoliu heard a horse whinny somewhere behind. He kept his eyes straight ahead. They passed a goat farm and then headed down a path running alongside the Oujiang River. Finally, they looked back. A few peasants were on the road and some children were playing down by the riverbank. No one else was around. The two ducked into a wooded area. Exhausted, they slumped down and then wearily began passing the gourd back and forth, drinking from it and washing cuts and scrapes.

For a moment, Baoliu studied the boy. He was dark-skinned, and probably a little older than him. He looked tough, almost mean. A thin scar snaked up the back of his neck and into his shaved scalp. His hands were rough, his feet splayed and so callused it looked as though he were wearing sandals of thick dirty skin. His clothes were homespun and had been patched so often with odds and ends of cloth that he seemed to be wearing a quilt. From a loop in his belt dangled a *daozi nonfang,* a peasant's knife.

"Thank you," said Baoliu, rubbing sore knuckles. "I wouldn't have had a chance without you."

"Wasn't anything," said the boy. "Just a favor returned."

"What's your name?"

"Zhou. Wanlun Zhou. You?"

"Baoliu. Where are you from?"

He shrugged. "Everywhere and nowhere. Yunnan province, that's where I was born." He scowled. "The plague of 1194 killed most of my family. Only my little brother, Po Sin, and I survived."

"Your brother—where's he?"

"Dead, too."

"I'm sorry," said Baoliu. "What happened?"

"The guards at a prison killed him, *that's* what happened," said Zhou, his voice filled with hate. "The bastards, they—" he began, and then shook his head. "I really don't want to talk about it."

Baoliu nodded. "How do you get by?"

"I do what I can, take what work I can get." He shrugged. "Someday I'd like to learn a trade. But for now, I do slopwork." Hard eyes fixed on Baoliu. "You've been in prison," he said.

"How did you know *that?*"

Zhou pointed. "The shackle marks on your ankles and wrists. What were you locked up for?"

"Theft," replied Baoliu, avoiding his gaze.

He puffed a laugh. "But you're a rich boy. Why would *you* need to steal anything?"

"What makes you think I'm a 'rich' boy?" asked Baoliu, suddenly nervous.

"Your hair, it's shaved back from the forehead. Only rich boys have their hair like that." Zhou frowned, seeming to look right through him. "And those boys. They didn't say anything about a robbery. They said you murdered someone. Who?"

"No one."

Zhou shrugged.

"The one who pushed me, he said that someone was executed in your place. Is that true?"

There was nothing else he could do; he asked Zhou not to repeat any of it and then told him everything.

"A *ka-di*," Zhou muttered when Baoliu was done. "How strange! I've never known a rich boy before—and you're one whose father bought his head!"

"If I'm ever convicted again—of any crime, I'll be re-tried and executed."

"You walk the razor's edge!" said Zhou, scratching a thin stubble of beard.

Baoliu nodded.

"What are you going to do now?"

"Don't really know."

Zhou looked up at the sun. "I've got to get going—to the docks," he said, gathering his things together. "Day's half gone. The docks, if you want to come?" He let the question dangle.

"I don't know," said Baoliu, feeling tangled up inside, not sure of anything.

Zhou shrugged, hefted his pack. "Well, good luck."

Baoliu watched as the boy headed away. Then he got to his feet suddenly, feeling as though he was being abandoned. Panic welled up inside of him. "Wait!" he yelled.

Zhou looked back at him. Baoliu took a few tentative steps.

The boy half-smiled, and motioned for Baoliu to come.

HEADED TO THE docks, Baoliu grew more and more certain he'd be recognized again, and worried out loud what to do about it. Zhou produced his knife, and then down by the banks of the Oujiang he shaved Baoliu's head. The two then exchanged a few pieces of clothing, some of Zhou's coarse rags for Baoliu's bloodied clothes. When they had finished, Baoliu looked in a mirror of burnished bronze. A baldheaded stranger looked back at him.

"*Gongxi ni, Baoliu!*" Zhou laughed as they headed off again. "Congratulations! You are now a peasant!"

BAOLIU HAD BEEN to the harbor area only twice before, once with his father and once with his brother, both times in a sedan chair.

Now he was on foot, and the place was even more awful than he remembered it: the stench of fish and rotting garbage; the babble of voices; the slop and splash of the sea. Revolted, he followed Zhou across the heavy planking of the crowded wharf to where a group of old men had gathered, sitting in the sun on bales of hemp.

"We need day-work," Zhou told them.

"The best jobs go at dawn," said a weathered little man. "But often there is work with the fishing boats that set sail early and then return in time for the afternoon markets."

Within the hour, Baoliu was hurrying after Zhou in the direction of a fishing scow being tied up at the dock. Quickly he found himself amid droves of boys descending on the dilapidated boat. They clamored for work, shouting to a tall man in a greased leather apron.

"*Ni!*" "You!" the man said again and again, pointing to the boys he wanted.

Zhou was one of the first chosen.

Baoliu was never given a glance.

"That's all," said the man.

Baoliu stood there stunned, outraged that he'd been passed over, and then felt a hand on his arm.

"Follow me," said Zhou, leading Baoliu toward filthy-looking worktables. "He'll forget who he picked. They always do."

Boys carrying a two-handled basket began spilling fish onto the tables.

"Get to work!" snapped the man in the apron.

Baoliu followed the lead of the others.

One after the other, he grabbed a slithering fish, some alive, some dead, and hacked off the head with a cleaver. He gutted it, and then passed it to a "salt girl," a child who washed the carcass in a bucket of water, salted it, and wrapped it in a lotus leaf.

"Kuai!" "Faster!" The man paced, grousing at them, watching them work.

Speed was everything. As soon as a salt girl had filled her basket, she would rush off with it to the market-place.

The task was not entirely new to Baoliu. As a boy, he'd gone fishing with his father and brother, and afterward they'd had to clean the fish. But this was very different. The sheer number of fish was impossible and the pace was exhausting, for as soon as he finished with one fish, he immediately went to work on another.

By day's end, Baoliu was thoroughly miserable. His naked scalp stung. From being in prison and from all that had followed, he was bruised and sore all over. But it was the work that had been almost beyond his will and endurance: from the almost nonstop butchering, his back and shoulders ached; his hands and clothes were wet with slimy red gore. He and Zhou washed up as well as they were able to in buckets of water behind the worktables and then wiped their hands and faces with pieces of mulberry paper.

As he finished cleaning up, an overpowering feeling

swept over Baoliu: he wanted to go home. He had been through so much—more, truly, than he ever had in his life. And now it seemed only fair that he be allowed to go where he belonged.

He heard the clatter of coins.

The tall man paid Zhou and Baoliu their wages: seven tongqian. The round coins with a square hole in the middle were dropped into Baoliu's outstretched hand. Zhou was pleased with the amount. To Baoliu it was an absurd pittance.

"This is all we get for so much work?" he blurted.

"How much did you think they'd pay?"

"*More than this!*"

"You don't look like a rich boy—at least not anymore." Zhou looked him up and down. "Now try to stop acting like one."

Baoliu scowled at the coins in his hand. "Where will we get something to eat with so little?"

"Don't know yet," said Zhou, heading away, gesturing for Baoliu to come.

Not far from the wharf, steam rose from a dilapidated food stall, one where other boys were eating. For two tongqian, a skinny little woman and her daughter doled out bowls of rice and small cups of tea. Not until he sat down with Zhou against a wall did Baoliu realize that the rice was gray and gritty-looking.

"What's wrong?" asked Zhou. "The dirt?"

"Among other things."

"I've eaten far worse," said Zhou. He scooped up the gray mess with two fingers and ate hungrily. "There have been times when I was sure I was going to die. I would have given anything for rice, even rice as poor as this." A faint sneer became a laugh. "Eat up, rich boy!"

Baoliu cursed under his breath; he ate, washing down each bite with a sip of tea. He thought of home, of the abundance of food. All the aromas and tastes—he tried to remember them, and then winced as something dug into his gums, and he spit out a pebble.

After finishing up, they rinsed their bowls and cups, returned them to the stall, and then headed into the darkening portside district.

"Where's a place to sleep for the night?" Zhou wondered out loud. "You wouldn't know, would you?"

"No." Baoliu looked at the gathering gloom of dusk and then around at the warren of desolate dwellings they were passing. "I know as little about this part of Yongjia as you do."

Kids came running happily and noisily down the unpaved street, rolling and chasing a bamboo hoop, playing some sort of game.

"*Ni Hao!*" "Hello!" Zhou approached a man standing in the doorway of a tilted-looking brick hovel. He asked about places to stay for the night.

"How much money do you have?"

"Four tongqian apiece," said Zhou.

"There are *wo-pu* that way." He pointed up the street. "One of them is very big. You can't miss them."

"A *wo-pu!*" said Baoliu with disgust.

"Would you rather sleep in the street?" asked Zhou as they headed up the cobbled path. Light gleamed eerily from doorways and windows. People passed in the darkening gray of twilight, some carrying lanterns. A woman sat huddled in a quilt, a baby at her breast. She held out a hand.

"I'm sorry," said Baoliu.

Before, in a life that suddenly seemed long ago, he probably would have given the woman a few tongqian without thinking about it. Now he was not much better off than her.

When he was a little boy, Baoliu had traveled with his father to Zhuzhou. Along the way they had stopped at taverns with good food and clean, comfortable quarters. He was still carrying this vision in his head as he found himself approaching what at first looked like a wall of people in boxes.

A sign on a warped board read: WO-PU—THREE TONGQIAN.

The long wood and bamboo building consisted of dozens of sleeping berths, many of them already occupied. In the growing dark, woeful faces gazed out from some; the bamboo shutters of others had been closed, allowing a degree of privacy. A fat, grubby-looking man took their money; three tongqian entitled them to one of the cubbyholes, a half tongqian to a blanket. Zhou took the first unoccupied berth they came to; Baoliu found another a bit farther on.

Cold, he crawled into the wretched place, feeling as though he were crawling into a coffin. It stank. *He* stank, mostly of fish. The blanket of padded quilting was stained and dirty. He pulled it around himself and lay down. Though he was exhausted, the place was so wretched and his mind so knotted up with black thoughts that he knew he'd be unable to sleep. He started thinking of his own soft bed at home.

The next thing he knew, it was morning.

6

SOMEONE WAS PUSHING on his arm.

"Rich boy," Zhou said, yawning. "Time to go to work."

"Quit calling me that." Baoliu groaned.

"Calling you what, rich boy?" He laughed.

Baoliu made a face and gazed out from the berth at a gray, sodden-looking morning, every part of his body aching. "Give me a few minutes," he told Zhou. "I hurt so bad."

"Quit whining and get going," said Zhou, annoyed. "You're holding me up."

Grimacing, Baoliu crawled from the berth, dragging the blanket after himself. He wrapped it around his shoulders and then found himself shivering awake, following Zhou and a line of dirty, unsmiling men toward an exitway. Not until he returned the blanket to the manager of the *wo-pu* did the full shock of the cold hit him. Zhou wore a heavy goatskin jacket, and Baoliu found himself staring enviously at it.

"Cold?" Zhou knelt down and pulled a quilted vest from his pack and tossed it to Baoliu.

"Thanks," he said, pulling the vest on over his stinking shirt. The thing was old and frayed, but it was warm.

At a food stall, they had a breakfast of bean-curd soup and tea and then headed down a long, well-traveled path to the harbor.

They found no work on the docks. But on the beach, in a large, open-air shanty, an old man with a long white beard gave them a job repairing fishnets. The walls of the place were draped with nets, a rising sun decorating the inside with a crosshatch of shadows. The place was peaceful, and Baoliu didn't mind the work—splicing thick strands of torn hemp together. It reminded him of making a woven mat with his mother, something they had done together shortly after she had gotten sick.

It had been more than a year since she had first begun showing signs of the wasting disease. At first, she had tried not to let it get the better of her; she still ran the house and oversaw the servants, and she still loved working in the garden and making flower arrangements for the house.

But soon she had begun to weaken, and took to lying on a blue divan in the front room most of the day. Within weeks she had taken to her bed. Friends and relatives came to see her, some from as far away as Shanghai, and Baoliu and Hai Nan and their father were constantly in and out of her room.

Sometimes for hours, Baoliu and his mother would talk. Once she told him about a fire that had destroyed most of Beijing when she was a little girl. She reminisced about her days serving in a duke's household, then of marrying Baoliu's father in Hangzhou—an arranged marriage, one in which the two did not meet until the day of the wedding.

She told Baoliu about how awkward it had been at first, but then how she had found herself falling in love with their father, and what a good man he had been and what great pride and pleasure he had taken in his work. They had been poor, but they had gotten by, happy in their determination to improve their lot in life. And they had done so. Throughout Yongjia, their father had become well known for his exceptional workmanship, and orders for the footwear he crafted had soared. He had purchased a much larger shop, and for a time they had lived there, in an apartment above the workplace, until they had moved to Tiantang.

In the end, she had spoken only of her love for her husband, her sons, and the rest of the family. For them to be happy after she was gone, that had been her only wish.

Each day, she had grown weaker, and her face had become narrow and shrunken-looking. Her eyes had seemed to grow large, and looked shiny and watery.

The family physician had visited daily. He tried to stop the illness with cauterization, massage, arsenic, and medicines made from plants and insects, but she had only gotten worse. To ease her pain, he applied acupuncture—until her body looked like a forest of needles. For a time, she seemed better, but then her pain became unbearable. She was given opium, in increasing amounts. And then mostly she slept.

One afternoon, Baoliu sat with her as she dozed. She smiled at him and squeezed his hand. A few moments later she was gone.

At the funeral, Baoliu and Hai Nan had held on to each other and wept. And their father had come to them; he had put his arms around them and told them to be strong.

But it was their father who had been weak, it seemed to Baoliu. He had turned cold and bitter. He was harsh with the servants. The slightest thing made him angry; strangely, it seemed that he was angriest with his wife, as though by dying she had abandoned him. He complained incessantly about how empty and lonely his life had become.

Less than four months later he had purchased Jia Lam.

"This murder that you were convicted of," said Zhou, startling Baoliu from his reverie. He looked up, a splicing knife in hand.

"Your father paid for your life to be spared but didn't speak up for you at your trial. Why? It makes no sense." Zhou rocked back on his heels, squinting at Baoliu through squares of shadow.

"Because he thought I was guilty—and wouldn't dishonor himself by saying otherwise in court."

Zhou smiled crookedly. "Rich people, they're so strange. A poor person couldn't afford to think like that!"

Baoliu shrugged, not knowing what to say.

"The crime—the murder—if you didn't do it, then who did?"

"I don't know. Could have been anybody."

"How about your brother?"

"It's possible. But why would he be stealing? He wasn't desperate for money—not that I know of. He gambles a little, but that's about it."

"Maybe he gambles more than you know? Maybe he owed money and was a lot more desperate than you realize?"

"I don't know. It's possible, I suppose. But I doubt it."

"How about a servant?"

"Some of them, perhaps, but not the house servants—they could have stolen anything they wanted at any time they wanted; they wouldn't have needed to sneak around at night." Baoliu shrugged. "Most likely it was just a common thief."

Zhou scratched the scar on his neck. "If that's the case, then whoever it was would have tried to sell the jewelry. And if you can find out who did, then you'll know all you—"

"You're a genius!" exclaimed Baoliu, interrupting him. "They would have tried to sell the things, probably to a pawnshop. If we can find out who sold the jewelry, then we'll know who killed Jia Lam!"

"Now, why didn't *I* think of that?" Zhou laughed.

THAT AFTERNOON, THEY headed into town, first to letter-writing booths near the town square. There, for two tongqian, illiterates dictated letters to scribes. For a half tongqian, Baoliu purchased a sheet of paper, quill and ink, and the use of a writing table.

"I don't even know what was taken," he admitted to Zhou. "But I'd recognize most of the pieces, especially the newer ones; they all had our family emblem worked into the design." He bent over the writing table, and as well as he was able, drew a picture of a snake biting its own tail.

The first pawnshop was just across the way. It had been built of the same material as the plaza's cobblestone pavement, and the place seemed to grow right out of it.

"*Mei Kanguo!*" "No!" said the owner, his face as round and hard as the stones that seemed to make up most of the strange shop. "No. I've not seen such jewelry. Now, out of here!"

Down the road they found a place selling used clothing

and jewelry. The owner there seemed intrigued by the question; the elderly lady, an abundance of combs in her white hair, studied the pictures at length. But then shook her head no and returned the drawing.

A man with gold teeth yelled at them and chased them out of his shop with a club. A young woman showed the drawing to other family members, but none were familiar with the design. A man and his wife, both of them very fat, gave each of the boys a fen, but had no information to offer. Some people treated them well, some treated them rudely; it made no difference: none knew anything about the jewelry.

From the heart of the city, the *Genggu*, The Drum of Time, began pounding, signaling the beginning of the last hour of the day.

Doors and shutters banged closed; iron screens were dragged across storefronts. People poured from workplaces. Across from Baoliu, a skinny water porter lowered the burden from his back, sat wearily on a doorstep, and then bowed his head, as though in thanks that his day was done.

"We'll try again. We probably haven't been to more than half the places," said Zhou as they headed back down through the city, the streets beginning to crowd with people headed home.

Suddenly, Baoliu stopped and stared. Wearing the black skullcap and a full-length robe of a merchant, his brother walked right past him.

"Hai Nan!"

"What?" He flinched, turned around. "Who are you?"

"Your brother."

"Baoliu!" He looked him up and down. "I . . . I'm glad to see you," he said, fumbling over his words. His eyes traveled to Zhou.

Zhou met his gaze and then gave Baoliu a knowing look. "I'll meet you at the *wo-pu*," he said, and with a backward wave headed down the street.

"Rangkai!" "Out of the way!" a man pushing a wheelbarrow grumbled, trying to get past them.

They moved to the side of the road, and looked at each other. Baoliu was in too much shock to know where to begin, and the same was true for Hai Nan, it seemed.

"Shall we walk?" he said.

They joined the flow of pedestrians headed up the street, saying nothing, just moving along with the others. Finally, a burned-out area beside the road offered an escape from the noisy throngs. Tall grass had sprouted from the blackened remains of a house that had burned down, seemingly not long ago; the pungent scent of burned wood still lingered in the air.

Tired-looking, Hai Nan sat down on the remnant of a wall. In the ashes, Baoliu spotted a small statuette of Buddha, and picked it up. Once white, the ivory Buddha was charred, the base of it almost completely burned away. He studied it for a moment and then dropped it back into the ashes. A tiny geyser of gray powder popped up.

"How have you been?" Hai Nan touched the filthy sleeve of his shirt. "How are you getting by?"

"I manage."

Hai Nan looked at him appraisingly. "I didn't recognize you at first," he said. "Your clothes. The shaved head. "

"How's Father?" asked Baoliu.

A noisy oxcart, one with massive wooden wheels, drowned out any other sound. They waited for it to pass.

"How is he?" Baoliu asked again.

"Not well."

"I'm sorry to hear that."

"He's tired all the time, and hardly has any appetite. He has trouble sleeping and often wanders the house at night. All that's happened—all these 'difficulties'—they have been very hard on him."

"I understand," said Baoliu.

"I don't think you do." Hai Nan crossed his arms into his sleeves. "Father has lost his wife. He has lost a son. And now he may lose his business."

Baoliu blinked. "Why?"

"It cost him eight thousand tongqian to save your life, much of his savings. But even worse, now he's losing customers. Because he's in disgrace, many of his best customers no longer come to the shop. And there's talk that his contract with the military may not be renewed."

"And this is my fault?"

"Yes," said Hai Nan evenly. "Who else do you think is to blame?"

"The person who killed Jia Lam."

"Ah, yes! The mysterious person that no one but you saw!" Hai Nan shook his head. "The constables questioned people for miles around, and asked if anyone had been seen running away that morning. None had."

"Perhaps the killer never fled."

"What do you mean?"

"That whoever killed Jia Lam may have been someone in the house—someone who belonged there, and had no reason to run away; they would have simply slipped back into their quarters." He looked Hai Nan in the eye. "Someone such as yourself."

"You're suggesting *I* killed her? How dare you!"

"It's possible."

"And why would *I* want to?" he snapped, getting to his feet.

"I have no idea. I only know that I didn't."

"You still claim to be innocent when so clearly you're not?"

"I *am* innocent. And as I told Father, I'll prove it someday."

"I hope you do."

"Do you really?" Baoliu scoffed.

"Yes, for your sake as well as ours. Do you think this is what Father wants for you? Do you think it is what *I* want—to have my only brother wandering the streets like some beggar?"

"I wouldn't know. All I know is that neither of you spoke for me at my trial, and not once did either of you consider the possibility that I was telling the truth!"

"We have! But nothing supports your story. Damn you, Baoliu, don't you think that Father and I care about you, that we would love nothing better than to see you prove your innocence? You would be welcomed back into the house. You would become part of our lives again. And once again the family name and business would be restored."

"Ah, yes, 'the family name and business'—that would be of the utmost importance!"

Hai Nan scowled. "Do you ever think of anyone but yourself? Do you care at all about what you have done to anyone else? What you have done to our family—to Father? Suddenly his whole world has been destroyed."

"I can't imagine what that would be like!"

"Does it matter at all to you that his life's work, his business, is about to fail because of you? Because of all this, we may lose everything!"

"How terrible! You could end up living in the streets."

Hai Nan stiffened.

"And I certainly wouldn't want that to happen!" Baoliu laughed. "The two of you might end up sleeping in the same *wo-pu* as me!"

Hai Nan glowered, clenching his jaw. "I'll tell Father we met."

"Do as you please."

Hai Nan looked at him sourly, and then shaking his head, turned and walked away, burned debris crunching underfoot. He glanced back at Baoliu for an instant and then continued on his way.

7

ALONE, THE NEXT day Baoliu went to every shop he thought they had missed. And he went to the street peddlers, those selling jewelry from carts and stands, and from mats spread on the ground. But again and again came the answer he expected—no, they hadn't seen anything on the order of what he was looking for.

"I'm not going to find them," he told Zhou the following morning as they headed down to the harbor area. "We've gone to about every place possible and haven't found anything. There's no place left to look for the jewelry, and I have no idea what else I can do. Maybe I should just start trying to put all this behind me."

"Maybe you should—I don't know," said Zhou, as they stepped onto the docks, and into fog drifting in from the sea. Gulls circled, jabbering and squawking as they followed boats headed out to sea.

"You two want work?" A man loomed out of the mist, and gestured to a huge trawler, the vessel rocking in the backwash of passing boats.

"Doing what?" asked Baoliu.

"Unloading the catch."

"How much?" asked Zhou.

"Eight tongqian until the job's done."

"Ten," said Baoliu.

"I'll give you nine, but no more." With a nod of agreement from them both, the man led them to the trawler and set them to work. In the trawler's hold was a small mountain of fish. Over and over, they filled large, two-handled baskets, hauled them across the dock, and then spilled them onto worktables for cleaning.

By the time they had finished, the day had turned hot and humid. Wet with sweat, every part of them coated with silvery-looking slime, they made their way down to the beach—and then walked right into the ice-cold sea, fully dressed, washing themselves and their grimy clothing at the same time. They made their way out deeper and deeper, until the water came up to their chins. And then, as fast as they had rushed in, they turned and hurried back, unable to bear the cold any longer.

"That felt good!" exclaimed Zhou, hugging himself and shivering as they trudged ashore.

"I don't think I've ever been so filthy," said Baoliu, following Zhou's example of stripping down to his loincloth and then laying out his clothes on a large, sun-heated rock to dry.

Baoliu looked down at himself, at an assortment of bruises and scrapes, and at hands so darkly tanned he seemed to be wearing gloves.

"Sometimes I wonder," said Baoliu, sitting down beside Zhou.

"Wonder what?"

"What would have happened if I'd never met you."

Zhou laughed. "You'd probably be dead by now."

"Could be." Baoliu shrugged. "And without my father, I'd be dead for sure. Instead, I end up sitting there in front of the whole world, watching a man have his head chopped off—with everyone wishing that I was the one down on my knees. As long as I live, that's the way everyone's going to see me."

"You sure you want to give up on trying to prove you didn't do it?" Zhou squinted into the glare of the sun.

"No, I'm sure I *don't*," said Baoliu. "Just as I'm sure I don't know what to do next; I have no idea how I can prove I didn't kill Jia Lam. All the evidence is against me; everyone is certain I killed her, everyone is sure I'm guilty, and there's nothing I can do about it. I can't prove anything to anybody. I'll just have to accept it and try to go on from there." He smiled grimly. "It's strange—sometimes I feel like I *am* guilty."

Zhou looked up.

"Not of killing Jia Lam but of killing Shen Manfong."

"Your father's employee—the one who was executed in your place?"

"That day in the execution yard, in my mind I keep seeing it. I keep seeing his head lying in the dirt. For what? He didn't deserve to die any more than I did."

"That's true."

"I wonder what he was like and what was going on with him." Baoliu bit at his lip. "Even if I can't clear myself, maybe I can find out what drove him to do it."

"You said he worked for your father. He was a shoemaker?"

"No, a tanner. He cured hides. He wasn't around much, maybe once every few months when he brought hides from one of our tanneries. He scalded himself—his hands—while working out back, behind the shop. I wasn't there. I just heard about it the next day. A long time passed. And then one day Shen Manfong came into the shop and walked right past me. I saw his hands. The scars were awful; some of the fingers looked as though they were webbed together."

"Then what happened? What'd he do?"

"I heard Father arguing with him in a back room."

"About what?"

"I couldn't make out what they were saying." Baoliu shrugged. "A while later the door to the office slammed, and Shen Manfong walked off—and looked really angry. I never saw him again—not until the morning of the *ka-di*," said Baoliu. "And for a second the night before, in the room in the guardhouse where they took me to see my father and the magistrate. He was thinner, and his scalp was shaved. He looked a little different, but I'm certain it was him."

"You said Shen Manfong and your father fought. How did they go from fighting with each other to Shen Manfong giving his life to save you?"

"That's what I'd like to know," said Baoliu.

"Where did he live?"

"I don't know. But I can probably find out."

"How?" asked Zhou, and then realized the answer himself: "At your father's shop. He'd know."

Baoliu frowned. "But I'm forbidden to speak to him."

"I'm not." Zhou smiled. "I'll talk to him. All right?"

Baoliu didn't answer. He just looked at Zhou. "You're a good friend, Wanlun Zhou," he said. "You don't even know that I'm innocent. I don't have any proof. All you know is what I've told you."

"You're wrong," said Zhou.

"What?"

"I *do* know you're innocent."

"How can you be so sure?"

"You don't have any reason to lie to me. Besides, after

the execution, you stayed in Yongjia. If you were guilty, you'd have gotten out of the city as fast as you could, to somewhere where you wouldn't be known. Instead, you're still here, still trying to prove you're innocent, still trying to find out what happened. That's not what a guilty person would have done."

"I guess you're right," Baoliu agreed. "Thank you. I never thought of that."

BY MIDAFTERNOON, THEY were headed into town, picking their way along narrow streets squeezed between clusters of look-alike buildings, all with the same tiled roofs and oiled paper windows.

"Jin Haozi!" The words were coming at Baoliu. "It is *him*, isn't it?"

Baoliu froze inside as he realized they were approaching two people he knew—a mother and daughter. The girl, Tao-an, was pretty, and once he'd had a crush on her. As they passed, Baoliu looked at her, embarrassed. Her mother made the sound and motion of spitting; then the two hurried on.

Zhou put a hand on his shoulder. "Forget it," he said.

Baoliu wanted to scream. He wanted to run—hide his face. He kept expecting to hear the words repeated, and kept looking around, scanning the way ahead and glancing over his shoulder.

But no one else seemed to notice him. Not even people

he knew. He passed two sisters he'd known since he was a little boy, and even a former tutor. None of them gave him a second look.

They made their way through the main market-place. Familiar sounds. Familiar sights, familiar places: an apothecary offering everything from electric eels to cure insanity and snake venom to stop pain; a small stand selling beauty products; a chandler's, the sweet smell of candle wax emanating from the place. And next to it, dwarfing it, was his father's shop.

For a long moment, Baoliu stood staring at the long green building—breathing hard, his mouth dry.

"You all right?" asked Zhou.

"I'm fine."

They rattled through the beaded doorway; the pleasant aroma of leather and the rhythmic tapping of hammers greeted them—and the sight of a half-empty shop. Hai Nan, seated at a high desk, writing in a ledger, glanced up, his eyes growing wide with surprised recognition, and then looked to his father, halfway across the room, examining a half-finished sandal.

"Baoliu!" his brother exclaimed, both surprise and fear in his voice. "Why are you here? What do you want?"

"My substitute—where was he from?" he asked, his voice tight. "Shen Manfong, the man whose hands were burned. I need to find his family."

Hai Nan's eyes were averted. Baoliu followed his gaze—and saw his father approaching him. The tapping of hammers stopped. His father turned on the workers. *"Gankuai zuo!"* "Back to work!" he ordered.

Heads lowered. The gentle tapping resumed.

Baoliu's father studied Zhou for a moment and then, scowling, looked at his son. "What do you want?" he asked, his voice strained, unnatural.

Baoliu repeated the question, and was startled when his father responded directly to him.

"He lived somewhere in the Minkao district. I do not know exactly where. Nor do I know—or care—why you want this information. But now you have it. And now you will kindly leave."

He bowed.

Baoliu did the same. He looked at his brother, and then left with Zhou, angrily slapping strings of beads aside as they made their way out.

"Where's Minkao?" asked Zhou.

Baoliu opened his mouth to speak, and then looked away, clenching his jaw.

"What's wrong?"

"Everything. The way he spoke to me, the way he looked at me. And the business—with so few workers, things *must* be bad. And my brother, the whole thing. Everything's wrong."

"At least he spoke to you. It's more than you expected."

"He talked to me like I was dirt, like I was a stranger."

"Maybe," said Zhou. "But he wasn't exactly expecting to see you; he was shocked and still mad. But he talked to you. And you got what you came for; you got the information you wanted."

"Yeah," said Baoliu, exhaling noisily.

"Where's the Minkao district?"

"Minkao? It's about the worst part of Yongjia," he said, gesturing in the direction they should go. "It's a horrible place, on the outskirts of the city."

They backtracked through the marketplace and then followed a trail that led up through sparse, half-dead vegetation. A sick stench began to envelop them; alongside the trail stretched a deep ravine littered with garbage and trash of every sort.

The trail rose steeply, and they found themselves emerging into a wretched slum. Dirty, naked toddlers wailed. Chickens pecked for seeds in barren-looking soil. The smell of garbage, rot, and cooking food wafted over the dreary sprawl of sagging, dilapidated huts.

A misty rain began to fall.

"Do you know of a man named Shen Manfong?" Baoliu asked a tall woman trying to patch the roof of a shanty.

She eyed him suspiciously. "No, I've never heard the name," she said, and returned to her work.

They asked several more people; each time, the answer—and the look—was the same.

"These people know more than they're telling," said Zhou. "They're hiding something—or they're afraid of something."

The two made their way deeper into Minkao and began asking again, and finally got the answer they wanted.

"*Wo renshi ta.*" "I know him," said a scrawny boy of about twelve or so. He was kneeling over a stove—a small *huolu*—in a shed, roasting a lizard impaled on a stick. He looked up. "Shen Manfong is dead," he said. "He was a very brave man. He gave his life in *ka-di*—for his family. They left many days ago, and moved—to a much better place than this."

"Do you know where it is?" Baoliu asked, his heart suddenly racing.

The boy blew on the lizard. It was small and leathery-looking, and smoke rose from the thing. "For a tongqian I will take you there."

Baoliu nodded in agreement.

He examined the lizard and then took a bite of it. "Come," he said. "It's not far."

Eating as he walked, the boy led them into the misting rain through the maze of ramshackle huts, Baoliu and Zhou following on his heels. They crossed a footbridge and then found themselves emerging into a better part of the neighborhood, heading down a cobbled street lined with tightly packed shops and homes.

"That's it," said the boy, pointing through drifting curtains of rain at a small, two-story building of wood and bamboo. "That's where they moved."

Baoliu gave him the tongqian they'd agreed upon.

The boy nodded and then headed back the way he'd come as Baoliu and Zhou began walking toward the place.

A badly made sign read: SHEN POTTERY AND PORCE-LAIN. The downstairs was a shop, one that hardly looked open for business; the upstairs, like most places, the living quarters.

Compared to the wretched hovels in the Minkao district, the place was a palace.

"To get his family out of poverty. That's the only reason this man sacrificed his life," Baoliu told Zhou, as they approached the shop. "Maybe that's all there is to know." He took a deep breath and rapped on the door—and stood with Zhou, waiting for it to open.

"Nobody lives there anymore."

"What?" Baoliu looked over his shoulder at a little girl sitting in the doorway of an adjacent shop, and then caught a glimpse of the boy who'd brought them there, hurrying up the street. *"Ni!"* "You!" he shouted.

"Little wretch tricked us!" grumbled Zhou.

The boy glanced back, and then ran, disappearing into the fog and rain.

"Who lived there before?" asked Baoliu, approaching the little girl.

"Shen Linlin and her scary grandpa."

"What's scary about him?"

"He's got only one eye. But Linlin is pretty," said the

impish child. "And she gave me a pony doll, but then she went there."

"Where?" asked Baoliu, and then looked to where she was pointing, at a distant hillside, the sodden slope blurred by rain, decorated with ugly fans of debris.

"The ravine we passed," said Zhou.

"When did they leave?" Baoliu asked, and looked up as a man appeared in the doorway.

"*Nigei wo gunkai!*" he barked. "Out of here!"

Zhou put a hand on Baoliu's shoulder. "Let's go."

Baoliu nodded, and backed away, looking the man in the eye.

"Get inside, Xia," said the man, taking the little girl by the hand.

"Yes, Papa," she said, and hurried into the house. The door slammed.

Baoliu frowned. "Come on," he said as they turned and headed back the way they had come, heads bowed to heavy rain.

"WE'RE IN TROUBLE," Zhou whispered as they continued back through Minkao, on a muddy pathway between squat gray buildings. His voice was tight, worried. "We're being followed."

Baoliu glanced over his shoulder into drifting rain and caught a glimpse of several boys—and saw clubs in their hands.

"Don't look back!" hissed Zhou. "And do what I tell you!" His hand slid down to the knife in his belt.

Baoliu looked around desperately for something to defend himself with.

"They got us!" Zhou spat and pulled out his knife.

Ahead, three more boys emerged from an alleyway, leering, blocking their way.

Baoliu and Zhou froze, then backed away, turning in a circle—as the ragged, sneering troupe came closer, slowly surrounding them. Baoliu clenched his fists, and then spotted a paving stone and snatched it up.

"What do you want with us?" Zhou snarled, wagging his knife back and forth.

Everything seemed to stop. Baoliu saw a woman looking out a window—eyes wide, waiting, watching. Someone with a lacquered umbrella hurried past, looking back at them.

"Where are you two from?" The voice was behind Baoliu.

"What do you want here?" said a bony, bent-backed boy. "Why are you so interested in Shen Manfong?"

A boy with blackened, missing teeth came closer, a dripping length of bamboo held high.

"Huh?"

"We used to know him," said Zhou.

"Don't you lie to me!"

The bamboo rod flashed. Zhou yelped, reeled forward, grabbing his wrist as the knife spun away and clattered somewhere. A fist slammed into Baoliu's face, and knocked him reeling; hands grabbed him, tearing his shirt half off. He swung wildly, heaved the paving stone, and then grabbed hold of a scrawny neck as hands dug at him, pulling him sideways. A face loomed near; he chopped at it open handed.

Zhou yelled and cursed, and Baoliu caught sight of him falling and skittering through muck.

An arm went around Baoliu's neck, dragging him backward as an open hand speared him in the belly. Air exploded from his lungs. He gagged, fell to his knees, felt his money pouch being ripped from his belt. He tried to get up. A wet foot smacked into his face and knocked him sprawling. He rolled over into muddy water and lay gasping on his back.

"Stay out of Minkao. Don't ask so many questions," said someone above him. "It can be dangerous."

Baoliu looked up at black teeth.

Someone else walked past and stepped on his hand. Cursing, he rolled over and watched as the bunch headed away through the rain and then disappeared around a corner. He started to get up, and then sat back in water. He looked at Zhou, leaning against a wall, blood dribbling from his nose. "They get your money, too?"

"Yeah," huffed Zhou, struggling to get his breath. He wiped blood from his lip. "My pack, at least they didn't get that." He limped to where the thing lay in the mud. "Do you see my knife anywhere?"

Baoliu looked around, shook his head, and then realized it was right in front of him, half-buried in garbage. "Here," he said, and held the knife up as Zhou took it from his hand.

Baoliu ran his tongue over a chipped tooth and put a hand to where his side ached. His knee protruded from his pants, bloody and scraped raw. His shirt and vest were ripped open and hung in tatters.

"Guess they don't like strangers," mumbled Zhou, looking at him out of one eye, the other nearly swollen shut.

"It's more than that."

"Yeah, I know," said Zhou, rubbing his knuckles. "But right now, I don't care. The only thing that matters is that we've got no money, not even enough for a *wo-pu*."

Baoliu struggled to his feet. "We'll find something."

"Yeah, what?"

Miserable, they headed down a side street and then through a marketplace, all of it desolate, shuttered off from the world. More and more, in doorsteps and under awnings, they passed people who had camped out, many of them just shapeless lumps beneath layers of damp quilts and blankets.

For a time, the rain eased—then hit with renewed fury. It came in driving, drifting sheets. It hissed, poured in splattering waterfalls from eaves, and burst from downspouts, spilling away in snaking little streams. It soaked them, plastering their clothes to their bodies. They hurried, trying to keep warm.

They followed a twisting path, crossed a footbridge of old planks, and then found themselves on a trail winding between shacks built on stilts on the hillsides. Ahead, a stricken-looking crowd had gathered. A huge wedge of hillside had given way, taking a house with it; what remained of the place lay half-buried in mud in a culvert far below.

"You're all safe. That's all that is important," said someone in the crowd.

"I felt the house start to move." An old man squinted into the rain, telling his story. "I knew what it was immediately. I screamed to everybody to get out. Don't take anything. Just get out. That is what I yelled."

Neighbors and others began shepherding the family into their homes. A woman holding a wax-coated rain shawl over her head glanced at Baoliu and Zhou. For a moment, it seemed she was going to say something. Perhaps even invite them in out of the rain. A picture flashed in Baoliu's mind of sitting by a fire, having tea, maybe even some hot soup.

Pulling the shawl tighter around her face, the woman hurried away.

"Now what?" grumbled Zhou.

Baoliu wiped water from his face. "I don't know."

Hunched against the rain, they followed the muddy trail across an open stretch and then found themselves passing between endless hovels. Tendrils of smoke rose from some, disappearing into drifting sheets of mist. Faces gazed out at them, watching them pass.

As wretched as the places were, Baoliu wanted to beg to be let inside. Everything hurt and he was so cold. The sky seemed to be darkening. Fog drifted, mixed with rain; a depthless gloom settled over everything.

The roadway narrowed and then descended sharply.

"The garbage dump," said Baoliu, shielding his eyes from the rain and gazing into the ravine below Minkao. "That's where the little girl pointed when I asked where Shen Manfong's family is."

Zhou shrugged, and slinging his pack over his shoulder, led the way down a gentle slope and into the trash-filled ravine.

There was nothing better they could do.

They scrounged planks and propped them against a narrow overhang of rocks, then piled everything they could find on top—a length of filthy matting, a moldy rug, and oversized leaves ripped from an elephant ear plant. Groaning, they crawled into the clumsy lean-to. Zhou sighed and leaned back. Baoliu rested his head against his knees and closed his eyes, grateful just to be in out of the rain.

8

BAOLIU AWOKE A hundred times that night. Zhou snored. Water dribbled through their roof of trash. He tried to get comfortable but couldn't. His knee and jaw ached, and again and again, things stung him—insects and spiders, he guessed. He slapped at them, pinched and crushed them, and scratched under his clothes at itching lumps. Several times during the night he crawled out into the rain to try to wash away the filth and vermin, numb the stinging, and stretch his cramped muscles. And then he could only crawl back in for more of the same.

Toward morning, the rain stopped, and Baoliu drifted into a deep sleep. He heard Zhou leave.

Birds began to squall somewhere.

He opened his eyes onto a triangle of sunlight. Clawed feet hopped overhead. A blackbird settled on a gnarled branch, and triggering a shower of water and leaves, took off effortlessly.

His torn shirt hanging open, he crawled from the sodden lean-to and sat on a lump of rock. Zhou was some distance off, a long stick in hand and chasing something.

Baoliu groaned getting to his feet and headed down through half-submerged grass and heaps of trash.

Zhou waved, watched Baoliu for a moment, and then went back to what he was doing—trying to spear frogs with a stick. Already, one lay on a fallen tree trunk, its legs and head removed and its white belly flayed open.

Picking up a pointed scrap of bamboo, Baoliu joined Zhou in the hunt, chasing after frogs. There weren't many, and the few Baoliu spotted leaped away as soon as he came near. He managed to spear only one; Zhou collected six, and also a small rat.

"I'll clean the rest of them," said Baoliu.

"Yeah—good," Zhou mumbled, sitting down and handing him the knife.

The first frog he picked up was still half-alive, its eyes moving and its body inflating and deflating with spastic, feeble breaths. He stabbed it, and sliced off its head.

"Sorry," said Baoliu, "sorry I got you into all this."

"Don't worry about it," said Zhou, rubbing at a cut above a black eye. "It could've been worse."

"The ones who attacked us—what were they so afraid we'd find out?"

"I don't know," said Zhou. "The only thing I'm sure of is that people up in Minkao seem to know something we don't. And they're trying to protect Shen Manfong's family."

"From what? And why would they be living in a place like this? From the *ka-di*, they received four thousand tongqian."

"It doesn't make any sense."

"The little girl we talked to in Minkao," said Baoliu, "she said something about a girl named Linlin and her grandfather—a man with one eye. They're somewhere in this ravine."

"We can find them later. Right now I'm more interested in eating." He gestured toward the flayed frogs. "And finding some way to cook these things."

The two started looking around for dry firewood; there was none—everything was wet, saturated. They wrapped their catch in leaves, and after collecting their gear, headed down the ravine, where the rising sun was turning piles of sodden debris into steaming, stinking little mountains. From one protruded the legs of some large animal, probably an ox.

As they passed the remains of an abandoned shanty, an old woman dragging a wooden board passed them going the other way, a little girl in muddy clothes trudging along behind. Vacant faces looked out from a cave, and from somewhere ahead they heard voices, and the scent of smoke began to permeate the air. "There," said Zhou, pointing at a cluster of shacks, and started to head in the direction of the closest one.

"Wait," said Baoliu. "The frogs—maybe we can use them."

"Use them how?"

"I want to find the family, find out what's going on, and talk to them. Right?"

"But what do the frogs have to do with it?"

"'Bring gifts to your neighbor and you shall be an honored guest,'" said Baoliu. "It's something my mother used to say."

Zhou's brow furrowed and then he nodded. "Okay, I understand. You're saying that bringing food can get us through the door. But where's the door? Where do they live? We can't just start asking around; if these people are like the ones up in Minkao, we're going to end up dead."

"And we can't go looking for them, hoping we'll just spot them," said Baoliu. "How do we find out where they are without making everybody suspicious? People are going to know we're not from around here."

"Then how about using someone who *is*?"

"I don't understand."

"What we need," said Zhou," is someone to lead us to them."

"How are we going to do *that?*"

"By having someone take something to them."

"Such as?"

Zhou began rooting around in his pack and then plucked out his bronze mirror. "This might work. It's about the only thing I have that's worth anything."

"I'm still not sure what you're doing," said Baoliu.

"Stay here," said Zhou, and then headed toward the nearest shanty.

Baoliu watched as Zhou approached a woman at work behind the shanty, and then heard him say hello and saw the woman look up. For what seemed a long time, the two talked; Zhou handed her the mirror, and then with a backward wave headed back to where Baoliu waited.

"What did you tell her?" asked Baoliu.

"That the mirror was from the little girl you talked to, and that she missed the older girl—Linlin—a lot and wanted to give her a present. I told her I didn't know where the family lived and asked her to take it to them. Only thing I'm worried about is that the woman will just keep the thing for herself or sell it."

For several minutes there was no movement around the house, and the woman was nowhere in sight. Then she emerged into view and headed on foot down a path through a sweep of tall reeds and bamboo. She looked over her shoulder and then made her way up a gentle slope. A short time later she was headed back the way she had come.

"Let's go," said Zhou.

THE TWO FOLLOWED the same route they'd seen the woman take, and found themselves approaching a hovel on a rise beyond tall clusters of bamboo; an old man and a young woman crouched over a small cooking fire. They looked up as the boys came near, their expressions wary. The old man was missing an eye; the lid had been stitched closed.

"*Nimen yao shenme?*" "What do you want?" asked the girl, standing up. She wore a man's jacket and a tan smock—and her hand was on the hilt of a knife in her belt.

"We've got seven frogs and a rat," said Zhou and opened the leaf wrappings around his catch. "But we have no way to cook them."

"Where are you from?" she demanded, pushing her long hair back from a pretty but grim face.

"Up near the top of the ravine," said Baoliu. "We mean you no harm."

She looked into the eyes of both, and then slowly nodded.

"I have a lot here, but no way to cook it," said Zhou, again showing her the catch.

The girl looked closely at the meat. "For half, I'll cook it. And I have soybeans and rice."

"*Hao.*" "Good. Then we agree," said Zhou.

The girl took the bundle from him and began stoking the fire. "We have meat, Grandfather," she said over her shoulder.

The old man looked up wearily and forced a smile. His good eye traveled from Zhou to Baoliu. "You are without a home?" he asked, his voice a raspy whisper.

Baoliu nodded. "Yes."

"And what are your names?"

"Wanlun Zhou."

"Huang Baoliu," replied Baoliu, lying, saying the first name that came to mind.

"I am Shen Pang," he said, running a hand back through a mane of long white hair. "And that is my granddaughter, Linlin."

Baoliu exchanged looks with Zhou. *She's the girl who was on the hill at the executions!* he told himself. *The one who yelled, "Father!"*

"Where did you find the frogs?" she asked, turning sizzling strips of meat on an iron brazier.

"Up near the top of the ravine," said Baoliu, inhaling the aroma. Linlin turned her attention back to her cooking.

"You have a black eye." Shen Pang said to Zhou. "How'd you get it, son?"

"We were robbed."

The old man looked at him expectantly, as if waiting for more details.

"A street gang," said Baoliu.

Shen Pang leaned close and put a hand to his sunken, stitched-up eye. "Lost this fighting in the North. Dart from a blowgun—went right through the lid," he rasped.

Baoliu's gaze locked on the ugly, punched-in hole—a fleshy pocket filled with stitches.

"A sailmaker sewed the eye closed, and I got stabbed in the throat in the same battle, in Kaifeng. That's why my voice sounds as it does."

"You were a soldier?" asked Baoliu.

"Foot soldier for almost thirty years, in the war against the Jurchens. Been fighting my whole life." He hacked a cough and spat, and then lifted his shirt, showing off another scar, a long gash across his chest—pink and folded over in places, like a row of puckered lips.

"This all but finished me. My insides got torn up. A *baldhead* got me with a hook knife," he started saying, and then burst into a spasm of coughing.

"Grandfather—enough talk," said Linlin.

"I'm fine," he groused.

She turned her attention to a battered pot and stirred it, waving away the steam.

Baoliu watched Zhou watching the girl, and then gave her a long look himself. She was tall and slender, and her hair hung to her waist. She appeared to be only fourteen or fifteen, but acted older—serious, like a child taking on the role of an adult.

He raised his gaze. The sky was a cold, limpid blue, tinged black and fuzzy beyond distant hills. On a pathway between a scattering of shanties, a work gang headed up a trail. Below, in a sunken, trash-strewn swamp, a pig rooted around in garbage, a woman with a stick over her shoulder watching it. Near the bottom of the ravine, children swarmed over heaps of debris, looking for anything of use.

"Ah, we eat!" exclaimed Shen Pang.

A bowl of rich-looking stew was passed to Baoliu. He attacked the food. They all did; they ate ravenously, in silence. In minutes it was gone. A few bones in the bottom of the bowl were all that remained.

"Where are you two headed?" asked Shen Pang.

"The docks, probably," said Zhou.

"I worked on the docks myself when I was a boy," he said. "Worked for a time on a merchant ship, too, in the galley. The pay wasn't much but I had plenty to eat! The cook let us take almost anything we wanted. That cook—he was a funny man. There was one man he didn't like, a sailor who kept complaining about the food always being the same thing day after day. So one day he served him something special, a dead rat floating in soup!" Shen Pang laughed, and burst into a hacking cough, gagging and trying to get his breath.

Linlin put her hands on his shoulders. "It's time to get some rest now," she said.

"Yes, yes," he rasped, wiping bloody spittle from the corner of his mouth.

"Can we be of help?" asked Baoliu, as she took him by the elbow, trying to get him to his feet.

"Yes, thank you. If we can get him inside."

"I'm fine," huffed Shen Pang, as Baoliu and Zhou, their arms around his waist, helped him up the incline toward a mud-brick hovel.

Linlin held back a door hanging and ushered them inside.

The place was warm and musty. A candle burned dimly in one corner, and Linlin, looking ghostly, picked it up and poured hot wax into a container of some kind; the candle's flame came to life, brightening the room in wavering amber. With the one candle she began lighting others.

The place slowly came into focus. It was a single room, larger than it had appeared from the outside, gaps in the stone walls plastered over with gray-white clay. On a shelf near the only window was a tiny parade of ceramic animals—tigers, rabbits, monkeys, and horses, and in a corner stood a homemade-looking potter's wheel. There was a crude table of planks, and a ragged maroon floor mat covered most of the hard-packed dirt floor. A folding screen curtained off the back of the place.

"In here," said Linlin, moving the screen aside as the boys eased Shen Pang onto a sleeping pallet.

"A burden, that's all I am," wheezed the old man.

"You're not," she said quietly, and put a pillow under his head.

"Don't let me do this to you!" he uttered breathily. "It's only because of me that you're still here. Leave this place. The constables—they'll find you. You've stayed too long already. Please, Linlin."

"I'm not going anywhere," she said soothingly, running her fingers through his hair. "Now please, Grandfather, just rest." She bent down and kissed him on the forehead.

"You're a good girl, Linlin," he said wearily. "Please, I can't have anything happen to you. You've got to get away before it's too late." He kissed her hand and then lay back, breathing heavily. "Please, do it for me?"

She covered him with a quilt. "Just rest, Grandfather," she said, and then quietly made her way from the shack.

Baoliu and Zhou followed her out and then sat down with her by the fire.

"How long has he been ill?" asked Zhou.

"For a long time, almost ten years, ever since he last returned from the war. The wound in his chest—it never really healed. Some days he's so weak he can't even get to his feet."

"Is there anyone else to help you? Any family?" asked Baoliu.

"No. Not anymore. Once there were eleven of us.

But then we had hard times, and my aunts and uncles and cousins moved on to other places in search of work. That left just my father and grandfather and me."

"Your father?" asked Baoliu, exchanging glances with Zhou.

"He was executed in *ka-di*," said Linlin.

"Ah, is that so?" said Zhou, feigning surprise.

"He gave his life for us," she said, and then looked at him aslant. "You don't know of the *ka-di*? You've never heard of Shen Manfong?"

"No." Zhou lied. "We've only been in Yongjia a few days. We're from Hangzhou."

"When did your father submit to *ka-di*?" asked Baoliu.

"Only a few weeks ago."

"He must have been a brave man," said Baoliu.

"Yes. He did everything for his family. And not just in the end, but his whole life. He worked so hard. He gave us everything he could."

"What kind of work did he do?"

"He was a tanner. He worked for the same man—the same rich pig—for almost twenty years." She scowled angrily. "He never missed a single day. But he scalded his hands while he was cleaning hides. He was in terrible pain, and couldn't work.

"When his hands had healed enough, he asked his employer for work, any kind of work, but the pig didn't care. He just told my father he was no longer of any use, not with his hands as they were!" She bit at her lip, looking from Zhou to Baoliu. "My father wasn't of any use to him—until his worthless son was convicted of murder and sentenced to death. That's when Father offered his life in *ka-di*. The money was supposed to save us— Grandfather and my aunt and uncle and cousins—but we never saw any of it."

"None?" asked Baoliu.

"Each week we were supposed to get a hundred tongqian of the two thousand promised us."

"*Two* thousand?" Baoliu blurted out.

"That's a lot of money," said Zhou, his gaze on Baoliu.

"It would have been, but like I said, we never saw any of it."

"But why?"

"The magistrate said they owed us nothing, that they never had."

"But how could that be?"

"Because of some law."

"What sort of law?" asked Zhou.

She looked away, avoiding his gaze. "Something I'd never heard of before, something that didn't make any sense." She pushed her long hair back from her face. "I petitioned my grievance at the House of Law, and requested an audience with the magistrate, but was denied. I asked that my petition be sent to the provincial governor; when this, too, was denied, I said that I would petition the governor myself. That's when the trouble started."

"What sort of trouble?"

"The letter I wrote was either intercepted by the magistrate, or somehow he got word of it. I'm sure he did, because the same day I sent it we learned that constables were coming for us. We've been hiding down here ever since."

"How long has that been?" asked Baoliu.

"Two weeks."

"What was in the petition you sent?"

"I told what the magistrate had done to my family. And I told about some of the other things he's done."

"What?"

"The farmers who are bonded into slavery and forced to work their own land without pay. The women and girls in Minkao he takes as his concubines. The people he has had killed. The magistrate does as he pleases and the constables do his bidding."

"Your grandfather said he wanted you to leave," said Baoliu. "If they're after you, why don't you?" he asked, in the same moment realizing the answer.

"He's too ill to travel." She scowled. "The magistrate— he lives in an estate large enough for a hundred people, and everyone else, we have nothing. The bastard is even more revolting than Father's stinking employer and his stinking son."

"The son—did you know him?" asked Baoliu, his eyes meeting Zhou's.

"No, why would I want to know some sniveling little rich boy?"

"So you never met him?"

"No."

"I wonder what became of him," said Baoliu.

"Who knows? Probably back in his fancy house, happy as can be."

Baoliu nodded. "You're probably right," he said.

9

OFF IN THE ravine, a handbell rattled faintly, and then a second one sounded.

"Constables!" exclaimed Linlin, getting to her feet. "That's the signal; they're coming this way! Grandfather and I—we have to get out of here! Please, can you help me? I've got to get my grandfather!"

Shen Pang was already coming out of the shack, bent over and leaning on a cane.

"What do you want us to do?" asked Baoliu. "Where do we go?"

"Hurry," she said, leading the way as Baoliu and Zhou,

supporting the old man between them, followed her into a maze of bamboo.

"You're going to get killed," muttered Shen Pang under his breath. "All because of me."

"Quiet," she begged.

Baoliu looked back through a screen of bamboo, and then squatted down, watching as a constable on horseback emerged, heading up from the swampy area below the hovel. The man dismounted, ran his fingers through his long, greasy hair; he peered into the empty shack and then made his way down to the cooking stove. Putting a hand above the smoldering embers, he looked around. He smiled, his gaze coming to a stop on the thicket of bamboo.

Linlin grabbed Baoliu's arm. He looked at her, at eyes wide with fear, and then at the constable, sword in hand, making his way up the slope "What do we do?" whispered Linlin.

It was the only thing Baoliu could think of, and it terrified him. He gathered up an armload of sticks and scraps of wood, and with a glance at the puzzled expressions on the faces of the others, headed back through the thicket—and out into the open.

"*Ni shi shei?*" demanded the constable. "Who are you?"

"I live here," said Baoliu, struggling to keep his voice steady. And staring in revulsion at the constable—his nose had been cut off and had been reduced to swollen lumps of flesh surrounding a cavity in his face.

"Live here—with who?"

"My brother."

"And where's he?" The question hissed out of the hole in his face.

"Working on the docks today," said Baoliu, putting down the bundle of wood. "Is something wrong?"

"Shen Pang and Shen Linlin—do these names mean anything to you, boy?"

"No."

"Don't you lie to me!"

"I—" began Baoliu, as a gloved hand grabbed him by the chin.

"You're lying to me! *Everyone* knows who they are."

"All right," sputtered Baoliu, pulling free of the man's grip. "Yes, I know who they are. The daughter of the man who died in *ka-di*—and her uncle or grandfather."

"Where are they?"

"I don't know. Honestly, I don't."

"No, I think you do!"

Baoliu stared at a sword pointed at his chest. "I don't. I have no idea where they are!"

"You're sure?"

"Yes."

The constable patted Baoliu on the cheek and smiled. "You're sure?" he asked again.

Baoliu opened his mouth to answer—as a fist slammed into his face, knocking him sprawling.

"Tell me what you know!" The guard knelt on him,

pinning him and crushing his shoulders, and then pressed the blade of his sword to Baoliu's neck.

"Tell me the truth!"

"I have!" sputtered Baoliu, licking his bloody lips.

"They're in Minkao—probably down in this stink-hole. We *know* that. Now, where are they?"

"I don't know. If I did, I'd tell you!" Baoliu looked up at the hole in the man's face and then into his eyes—eyes that were searching his and deciding what to do. Then he felt the weight of the man rise off him.

"I find out you lied to me, you're dead. You understand that?"

Baoliu tried to nod. He tried to raise his head, but then lay back heavily, dizzy and struggling to get his breath.

"BAOLIU! ARE YOU all right?"

He felt Zhou behind him, lifting him to a sitting position. "Yeah," he managed to say, dragging a sleeve across his bloody mouth.

"That was some quick thinking!" said Zhou. "You paid a mean price for it, but it worked."

"Thank you, son," rasped Shen Pang, as Linlin helped him sit down. "If you hadn't done that, I don't know what would have happened!" He coughed, putting a hand on Baoliu's shoulder. "That was brave—it took real courage!"

Baoliu smiled his thanks.

Linlin knelt down in front of him with a bowl of water and began wiping blood from his face with a wet cloth. "I'm so sorry. This is all because of us."

"It's not your fault."

"No." Shen Pang huffed. "It's mine. If it weren't for me, you'd be far from here, Linlin. Safe somewhere!"

"Please, don't talk like that, Grandfather," said Linlin.

Pang gestured in the direction of Baoliu. "And look what he did to this boy. He almost killed him!"

"I'll be all right," said Baoliu, wincing as Linlin touched the cloth to a scrape on his chin.

"You don't *look* all right," said Zhou. "You're a mess."

Baoliu looked down at clothes hanging in bloody tatters and at mud-caked hands and feet. He realized Linlin was studying him.

"I'll be back in a moment," she said.

Baoliu watched her make her way into the shack, Shen Pang toddling in after her. He heard the two talking in muffled tones, and then looked up as Linlin emerged, a rolled bundle under her arm.

"Let me get this off of you," she said, helping him out of his ragged shirt. She tossed it aside and then wiped blood and dirt from his chest and hands. "I wish I had more to give you."

" 'More to give' me?" muttered Baoliu.

"Put this on," said Linlin, unrolling the bundle and holding up a shirt. "It's the least I can do. Let me have your hand."

"Thank you," said Baoliu, sliding a hand into a sleeve and pulling the shirt on.

"For what you did—he'd want you to have it."

"Whose shirt is it?"

She smiled somberly. "It was my father's."

"I WANT TO tell her. I have to," said Baoliu, watching as Linlin made her way back into the shack.

"You want to tell her *now?*" asked Zhou. "Now when she thinks so well of you?"

"Especially now. Everything's turning into some sort of strange lie. It's going too far. This shirt that she gave me—her *father's* shirt." He pinched together the fabric of a sleeve. "I'm wearing a dead man's shirt, a man who was executed instead of me!"

Zhou nodded, and glanced back at the shack, at the sound of muted quarreling.

"But it's not just the shirt," said Baoliu. "It's more than that."

"What?"

"The two of them, they're being cheated. My father paid eight thousand tongqian for the *ka-di*. Half was supposed to go to the government, half to the family—four thousand each. The magistrate told them they were to receive only two, and then tells them they're owed nothing!"

"The rich finding ways to get richer, taking everything

they can in any way they want—that's how it's always been," said Zhou.

"I understand, but I think there's even more to it than that. Something else is going on. The magistrate says they aren't entitled to anything. Why? What reason did he give?"

"I have no idea."

"How do we find out?"

"Not by telling Linlin who you are. If you do, you're not going to find out anything. She wouldn't have anything to do with you." He smiled. "She really likes you. Keep it that way."

"'Likes' me?" Baoliu shook his head. "She doesn't even *know* me!"

"Maybe she knows you better than you think."

"What do you mean?"

"What I'm trying to say," began Zhou, and then stopped himself as Linlin emerged from the shack and headed down toward them.

"Would you do something for me?" she asked.

"Yes—what?" asked Baoliu, looking up at Linlin's teary eyes.

"I have an errand to run. If you could watch my grandfather for me."

"Of course."

"I won't be gone long."

Baoliu nodded and watched as she headed away, and then glanced back at the shack. Shen Pang was standing in the doorway. He waved to them feebly, and then disappeared back inside.

WHEN LINLIN RETURNED, she was clutching a porcelain vial. "Thank you," she said as she passed Baoliu and Zhou. She looked at them blankly and then made her way inside.

"You know what she's doing, don't you?" asked Zhou.

"I wish I didn't."

"She's bringing him what he wanted."

"I know," said Baoliu. "Poison."

10

LINLIN EMERGED FROM the shack as though in a trance, and then sat down by herself on a ledge overlooking the ravine. Baoliu got up to go to her but then hesitated and looked at Zhou, who shook his head.

"She needs to be alone now," he said quietly.

Baoliu nodded. "And there's something we have to do," he said, and looked toward the hovel, exhaling through clenched teeth.

Inside, they found Shen Pang curled up beside a pallet, dressed in an ancient-looking uniform, medals hanging from ribbons around his neck. Green liquid stained his lips and an empty vial was gripped in a lifeless hand. A rigid eye stared at them.

Together, the two lifted Shen Pang onto the pallet and lay him flat, smoothing and straightening his uniform. Baoliu pressed Shen Pang's eye closed and wiped his beard and mouth. Zhou took the vial from his hand and then took his arms and put them at his sides.

"There's nothing more we can do," said Baoliu.

They stood, looking down at him—the uniform, the scars, the stitched eye, the beard and mane of long white hair.

"I wish I'd known him better," said Baoliu.

They bowed to him, praying hands to their faces, and then turned at the sound of the door hanging being pulled back. A strange-looking, stumpy little woman—a shaman—entered the shack. There was a ring in her nose, her arms were tattooed, and around her neck was a garland of bones.

Linlin followed her in. "This is Nin-Ue," she said, her voice strained. "She will attend to Grandfather. Could you assist her?"

"I will need you to make a bier, a carrying platform for the body," said the woman.

Baoliu nodded. He put a hand on Linlin's shoulder and then followed Zhou out the door.

In the vegetation beyond the shack, Baoliu collected lengths of bamboo as Zhou searched out raw hemp.

They cleared a place and then began lashing bamboo together into a crude platform.

Night had fallen by the time they finished. Together, they carried the makeshift bier down the slope and into the shack. The place was brightly lit—candles burned around the room and incense cloyed the air. At the back of the room, the shaman had finished washing the body and was redressing it.

"Come," she said.

They set the bier on the table and then, as the little woman guided them, they carried Shen Pang to it and lay him down carefully.

Bracelets rattling on her wrists, the little woman smeared a stripe of damp ash on Pang's forehead. She put coins on the lids of his eyes, and then placed a piece of jade in his mouth. And to keep the mouth closed, she pulled a cloth under his chin and knotted it atop his head.

"Death is not an ugly thing if it is a life fulfilled," said the woman as she finished. She smiled in a strangely warm manner. "Is it not so?"

"Yes," said Baoliu, wondering at the notion, watching as she put a hand on Shen Pang's shoulder.

"*Ni anxi ba.*" "Rest," she said.

FROM MOUTH TO mouth. From shack to shack. Word of Shen Pang's death spread that night throughout the ravine and Minkao.

In a dawn of fading haze, mourners began arriving. Two old women, both with flat, blank faces, arrived first.

A man on crutches followed. And then a girl with hardly any teeth, though she looked no older than Linlin. Monks in orange robes, their feet caked with mud, came in quietly; they chanted over the body, reciting sutras, the Buddhist prayers.

Several who came were elderly men, old friends, most of them fellow soldiers in faded uniforms, each of whom saluted Pang and then bowed to him.

Midmorning, the body was enshrouded in white and then tied to the bier. Shen Pang's friends hefted it onto their shoulders, headed out with it, and then picked their way slowly down a path through the ravine. Linlin walked behind them, and behind her trailed a small wake of mourners.

In a blackened, ash-strewn stretch of ground, children from the ravine were finishing preparing a funeral pyre. The procession halted for a moment, and then Shen Pang's body, blanketed with flowers, was laid on the large pile of branches and wood.

A silent crowd gathered around as an old man told of his boyhood with Shen Pang, and of what a good friend he had always been—and how much others had liked him.

A nervous little man spoke of Pang's belief in life eternal, and of how he had found it in his son and granddaughter. He then took Linlin's hand and stepped aside. For a long moment she stood desolate, as though stricken with fright. She wiped her eyes. Then slowly she raised her head, and summoned the strength to say a poem:

I weep for him,
And I am ashamed by the feebleness
Of my words.
A great man is dead.
Yet the children play.
The birds sing,
And the cool stream does not pause
For even a moment.
It is forever on its way,
Yet always here.

A tall man in a threadbare officer's uniform spoke last, and at length. "Pang was not just brave and strong and good," he said in conclusion to his thoughts, "Shen Pang was the rarest of things. He was an honorable man."

The pyre was lit. Standing with Linlin and Zhou, Baoliu watched as flames crawled up through the wood and then flowered skyward. Smoke puffed from the hollow ends of bamboo. Wood popped, collapsed. The pyre sagged, cracking apart, and then burst into a single blaze. The three watched for a long time, until only a few other mourners remained, and until the fire had diminished into a shapeless patch of glowing embers.

THE FUNERAL OF Baoliu's mother had been a darkly splendid affair—everything of the finest quality—ornate, impressive, perfumed by flowers and incense, and attended by scores of richly dressed men and women. After the service, everyone came to their house, mingling, speaking in hushed tones, sipping wine, and nibbling at delicacies.

Only a handful of mourners returned to the hovel after Shen Pang's funeral—poor people in worn and ragged clothing, Pang's old friends, and friends from nearby.

There were no delicacies, no rich platters of food at the gathering for Shen Pang. There was only weak tea and rice balls, and endless stories about the man: battles he'd fought, pranks he'd played, people he'd helped. A one-armed man was telling about the first time he'd met Pang when a handbell suddenly rang out in the ravine.

"*Nar!*" "There!" exclaimed a stoop-backed man, pointing at mounted constables racing across a distant field.

"They're coming this way!" yelled Zhou.

"Hurry!" Baoliu grabbed Linlin by the arm and was backing away with her when a single constable—long-bearded, in full armor—clattered out from a clump of bamboo below, and whipping his horse, urged it up the slope.

Mourners stood frozen in place, watching his approach.

"Ni Hao!" "Hello!" he chortled in mock greeting, glancing in the direction of distant hoofbeats, seeming anxious for the other constables to arrive. Reining in his horse, he began to circle the mourners. Whip in hand, his gaze traveled from face to face, and then fixed on Linlin.

A toothy grin spread open on his bearded face. "Ah!" he exclaimed with glee. "We've been looking for you!"

A woman wearing a dress made from a blanket stepped in front of Linlin. "Please leave the girl alone," she said fearfully. He laughed—and walked his horse into her, knocking her to the ground. And laughed again louder.

"Swine!" hissed the one-armed man.

"What?" the constable growled, raising the whip high overhead. "What did you say?" He slashed at the man—and missed, the whip cracking across the face of a tall boy, who reeled away and fell shrieking to his knees.

"Bastard!" yelled Zhou, grabbing at the whip, trying to wrench it from the constable's grasp.

"Get it!" screamed Baoliu, clawing at the man, getting hold of his collar and pulling him backward.

The horse wheeled, squealing as it rose up on hind legs—the constable crying out as he flew from the saddle. He landed heavily in a spray of gravel and tried to get up. Instead, he rolled onto his side and lay gasping, licking at blood-reddened teeth.

"Linlin!" yelled Zhou, trying to get control of the horse.

Baoliu grabbed her, and then with the help of the one-armed man, lifted her, trying to get her onto the saddle.

"More! More are coming!" a woman shouted, the mourners scattering, fleeing in every direction.

"*Xu!*" "Go!" shouted Baoliu, smacking the horse's hindquarters.

"No!" Linlin cried, grabbing the mane as the horse cantered sideways and then surged away.

"Baoliu!" yelled Zhou.

He turned—saw bloodred teeth—saw the constable stumbling toward him, sword in hand.

"I'll kill you!" the constable screamed, sword upraised—as Zhou tackled him, and then was on top of him, pounding at his head.

Over a rise appeared a constable, and then several more.

"Zhou!" shouted Baoliu, pulling him to his feet.

The two backed away together, and then, in terror, they ran.

11

THEY HURTLED DOWN a grassy hillside—fell, skidded on wet grass, and then were running again through a forest of twisted, half-dead trees.

They saw Linlin—staggering toward them, limping, holding her arm.

"The horse threw me," she muttered. "I—"

"Linlin!" Baoliu reached for her and then found himself stumbling after her and Zhou, splashing through ankle-deep water.

A chorus of hoofbeats was coming closer, getting louder.

They sank to their knees in a sump of debris and rotting vegetation.

Four mounted constables thundered past. "What do we do?" whispered Baoliu. "When they don't find us, they'll be coming back."

"There are caves," said Linlin. "Follow me."

They slogged through stagnant water, then stopped. Ahead lay open ground, and beyond was the face of a cliff, pocked with caves.

"It's not much farther."

"The bastards are coming back!" Zhou glanced over his shoulder at the sound of approaching men and horses. "Go!" he hissed.

They loped in a crouch and then broke into a run. Hoofbeats pounded closer. They leaped over a gully. And then they were scrambling up a slope together, tiny avalanches of dirt spilling behind them. Baoliu saw a stone break loose, then bound away with explosive bangs.

"Up there!" someone shouted far below.

"This way." Linlin panted and ducked under a stone ledge. Baoliu and Zhou hurried in after her—and found themselves in a vast cavern. The footing was soft and damp, and everything stank of urine.

"Bats," whispered Linlin. Baoliu looked up. The ceiling of the cave was a writhing tapestry of the creatures.

Baoliu pushed Linlin ahead of him, and then stumbled against her. She yelped, her cry whipping the bats overhead into a frenzy. A shrieking whirlwind suddenly descended on them, and then streamed away, looping upward and out the entrance of the cave.

"Keep moving!" gasped Baoliu.

They hurried on, across the rank footing, and then were weaving past boulders and in and out of dark passageways. On all fours, they crawled up a rocky incline, and emerged into another vast chamber, the ceiling sparkling with crystalline light, and studded with huge, fanglike formations.

Heavy footfalls echoed behind them, and then voices, muted and disembodied.

Baoliu looked back at fuzzy shapes moving through the darkness, far behind them.

They hurried on. Helping one another, they picked their way up an incline of solid stone. Then they walked, into pitch blackness, arms outstretched and feeling their way—running fingers along invisible walls. And then touching only space.

"Linlin? Zhou?" Baoliu whispered, and put his hand on the outline of Zhou's shoulder.

"Where are we?" Zhou murmured breathily.

"I don't know," said Linlin, "I've never been this far in before." Baoliu felt slick rock underfoot and then stepped into shallow water. His arm brushed something; he reached out, and touched cold stone. Something ran over his hand, something clawed, furry. A rat.

"We're lost. There's no way out," muttered Zhou.

"We'll find a way," said Linlin. The way descended into a deepening crevasse.

"We have to stop." Zhou huffed, but kept moving.

The footing turned to mud. Baoliu inhaled humid, reeking air. A wave of nausea swept over him. He felt too sick, too weak to go on.

"I have to stop." he said, and sat down where he stood, and heard the others settling down around him.

"It's hopeless," he said. He paused, and wearily hung his head. "There's no way out."

"We're going to die in here," said Zhou solemnly.

Baoliu sat back, hands flat to the cave floor. He looked up into the blackness, wondering at the flecks of light overhead. Only slowly did he realize he was gazing up into a patch of night sky. They had not looked up; during their dark wandering, night had come, and they were sitting in open air. As he blinked his eyes into focus, he could make out the silhouettes of trees and hills.

"I'm so sorry," said Linlin. "I've led you to your doom."

"It's not your fault," said Zhou.

Baoliu laughed. "Look up!" he exclaimed. Following his own command, he gazed upward into a starry night sky.

THEY PICKED THEIR way down a hillside through dark vegetation. And then they were hurrying along dikes, long, interconnecting pathways surrounded on all sides by rectangular patches of rice paddies.

Baoliu looked back through the dark; no one seemed to be following them.

"Where do we go?" asked Linlin. "What are we going to do?"

"We should head south, to Jinwo," said Baoliu. "I've been there. It's down the coast."

"How far?" asked Zhou.

"It's less than a day trip by sea. But on land? I don't know."

Ahead glowed a small village, five or six thatched huts, voices rising from them, magnified in the still, evening air. The three approached anxiously, following the only path, right through the village center. A farmer and his look-alike son; a group of children poking sticks into a cooking fire; a fat woman in the doorway of her shack—the people stared at them, wondering at the strangers passing through.

"Where did you come from?" asked a little girl.

"Back there," said Linlin with a tired smile, turning as she walked, pointing back at the dark landscape.

"*Zaijian!*" "Good-bye!" called the little girl as they hurried on.

They crossed a road and then headed across a black field of soft grass. It grew colder, the air misty; they inhaled the scent of the sea, and began to hear the redundant roar of it.

"Jinwo—it's about twenty li," said Baoliu as they made their way out onto soft sand, the sea looming black and glistening beyond. "We'll go as far as we can tonight, and then—?" He shrugged.

They hurried on, keeping to the hard sand between the water and the beach, breakers rumbling, white fans of foaming tide swirling toward them and then hissing away. Far out at sea, the lights of boats seemed stopped in blackness. Overhead, a full moon seemed to be following them.

They continued on, each step getting harder than the last, their pace gradually slackening, and finally slowing to an exhausted walk.

"We're all right—we've lost them," said Zhou, his voice a tired monotone. "We have to rest."

Above the beach they settled into a narrow cleft beneath a sagging canopy of vegetation. In dappled shadow, they looked at one another.

"We'll head out again in the morning," said Baoliu. "We're going to be fine." He smiled faintly and then curled up on a pungent bed of damp leaves. He pillowed his head on a hand, and then felt the pleasure of sinking into the oblivion of sleep.

SOMEONE WAS PUSHING on his arm. Baoliu blinked at sunlight streaming through the trees, and looked up at Linlin, framed in its glow. "Baoliu," she whispered, her face rigid, worried.

Zhou crawled past and aimed a finger through a fringe of sea grass.

Baoliu peered out. On a distant curve of coastline, mounted constables trotted—four of them, coming in their direction.

"Look." Zhou's voice was an angry hiss. "We led them right to us!"

"What?" asked Baoliu. And then looked out at the beach and saw it—a long trail of overlapping impressions in the sand—their own footprints! The trail stopped just below.

Zhou pulled his arm. "Let's move!" he murmured, already pushing back through dense foliage, scrambling after Linlin.

They broke through a screen of dead branches onto a broad ledge, leaped from it, and hit the ground running, racing after one another across an open field. They splashed through a shallow pond, and then were climbing, pushing their way up through thick underbrush.

Linlin yelped, and wiped at a bloody scratch on her hand. "I'm all right," she said.

Baoliu blinked sweat from his eyes, and then scrabbled after her.

Somewhere behind, a horse snorted.

"Which way?" Baoliu asked, as they came to a stream.

"Down." Zhou panted, easing into the water.

"They're coming." Baoliu motioned with his head

in the direction of distant hoofbeats, then caught a glimpse of constables wending their way down a hillside. "Let's go!"

They moved fast, in silence, knee-deep water pushing them from behind. The stream branched, and then branched again, and turned to a green film of stagnant, foul-smelling water.

"This way," said Zhou.

Single file, they made their way down a narrow pathway.

"What's that?"

Baoliu swept aside tall grass and looked out as a cart rattled past on a roadway—and then gazed down at a ship-cluttered harbor and a city that seemed squeezed between two towering cliffs.

"Jinwo," he said.

12

"WE HAVE TO keep away from the roads," said Zhou, easing back into the foliage.

Baoliu nodded, and then found himself following the other two back through the brush and then along a trail winding high above the city. It seemed to go on forever. Head bowed to a hot midday sun, he struggled to keep up, his legs rubbery, his clothes hot with sweat and plastered to his body.

Linlin and Zhou, looking no better off, stopped ahead and waited for him to catch up.

"Are you all right?" Linlin pushed back wet bangs.

He nodded, too hot and tired to speak. He pushed on.

The trail descended sharply, and a fragile breeze rose from somewhere below, cooling them. And carried on it were children's voices. Up ahead, a little boy ran past, and then picked his way out onto a rocky ledge; he yelled happily, and jumped.

Water exploded below, pluming upward.

Baoliu peered over the ridge—and looked down at a lake, a basin of blue water girdled by rock. In bunches along the shoreline, on patches of sand between rocky escarpments, people were sunbathing or swimming.

From a side trail, a little girl clambered up over a boulder, followed by an older boy.

"*Ni xian zou?*" she asked. "Would you like to go first?"

Baoliu patted the little girl on the head. "Yes," he said—and then stepped to the edge and jumped—grabbing his knees midair and then slamming into icy water.

He stroked to the surface and, treading water, watched as Linlin and Zhou jumped. He swam, feeling the sweat and filth washing off him. He gulped water, and then let himself sink; he dove underwater, and then rose back to the surface in an upwelling of bubbles. Looking back at Linlin and Zhou swimming toward him, he felt his foot touch bottom, and he walked backward in knee-deep water.

Little boys splashed past, chasing each other.

Linlin and Zhou sloshed up through the shallows.

Baoliu took Linlin's hand, helping her, and put a hand on Zhou's shoulder as they slogged ashore.

"*Hao shuang.*" Linlin smiled. "That felt wonderful."

"I feel like I just came back to life," said Baoliu, returning her smile.

"Yeah, it was great," said Zhou, looking around at the surrounding cliffs. "But we have to keep moving." He started up a rocky escarpment, looking back to make sure Baoliu and Linlin were following.

Beyond a tangle of fallen trees, they found a spot to rest, a grassy depression surrounded by trees and overlooking the lake.

"I think they've lost our trail," said Zhou, sitting down with the others. "Still, they're going to figure out that Jinwo is probably the first place we'd head. We've got to decide what to do. Do we keep going or stay here? Once we get into the city, into Jinwo, we're going to be hard to find. Still, like I said, it's one place the constables are sure to look. But if we keep going, we're going to be out in the open. We'll be easy to spot."

"We're probably better off in Jinwo, at least for a while," said Baoliu. "Then we can move on, if and when we decide to."

"I don't want to move at all," said Linlin wearily. "I'm not sure I'm capable of it."

"We'll rest," said Baoliu. "For now, we're probably as safe right here as anywhere else. Besides, we don't even know if they're still after us." He looked at Linlin. "Are they *that* determined to get you?"

"I'd be surprised if they weren't." She ran her fingers

back through damp hair. "The constables who are after us are probably some of the magistrate's private thugs, the ones he pays to do his dirty work. They're killers, and they won't give up easy."

"Didn't you say you sent a letter—a petition—to the governor?" asked Baoliu.

"Yes."

"What was in it? Was it *that* much of a threat to the magistrate?"

"It was a long, long list. I wrote about everything he's done—all the people he's cheated, all the ones he's had killed."

"Who's he had killed?" asked Zhou.

"Anyone who crosses him, anyone who speaks out against him."

"And you knew this when you wrote the letter?" he asked incredulously.

Linlin shrugged. "I was too mad and disgusted to care. I know what the magistrate's capable of, but somebody had to stand up to him." She grimaced. "Now I wish I hadn't—not because of what's happened to me, but because of what's happened to everyone else. The magistrate hurt a lot of people in Minkao trying to find me. And because of that letter—because of me—my grandfather is dead. He killed himself so that I could get away."

"It was what he wanted," said Baoliu.

"And I did the same thing to my father." She looked up, her eyes wet with tears. "He died to save me, too."

"It's not your fault," said Baoliu.

"No?"

"No, none of it is."

"If it isn't, then why does everyone I care for end up dead?" She looked from Zhou to Baoliu. "And the two of you—are you next? You saved me, just like my father and grandfather did. If you were smart, you'd leave me and head off on your own."

"We're both sort of stupid," said Baoliu with a half smile. "We're not going anywhere without you."

"You're stuck with us," said Zhou. "That's just the way it is. Sorry."

NOT UNTIL LATE the next morning did they start to rouse themselves. Waking up slowly, they sat together on a ledge, gazing down at the lake. A little boy walked along the shore, a dog trotting at his side. No one else was in sight.

"Where is everyone?" Zhou yawned.

No one answered.

Linlin stood up and then headed down the rocky slope, Baoliu and Zhou picking their way along behind. They knelt beside the lake, splashing water on their faces.

From somewhere below came the roar of a crowd.

"Something's going on," said Baoliu.

They headed down from the lake, following its winding shoreline, and then made their way along a well-traveled trail. Beyond a forest of reeds below, a sweep of tiled rooftops came into view. And then they heard a babble of voices.

"What's this?" said Zhou, as the path opened onto a busy street.

"A Festival of Lights, I think," said Linlin.

Paper lanterns hung from trees and the eaves of houses, and every house was festooned with paper streamers. The streets teemed with people, many of them soldiers and sailors. The wealthy rode on horseback or in covered sedan chairs. A delicate hand parted the curtains of one; an expressionless, heavily made-up face peered out at them.

Linlin grabbed Baoliu's arm. He stared.

A pair of constables trotted toward them—and then kept going.

"It's all right," said Zhou. "They're local. Their armor—the iron-ribbon tunics, the black helmets, the steel-toed boots—they're Jinwo constables."

"Still, they could be trouble," said Linlin.

"*Bikai!*" "Out of the way!" cried a woman carrying an oversize basket, trying to get past as a crowd began to back up behind them.

The three moved along with the others, all heading in the same direction.

"The Pleasure Grounds," said Linlin as they emerged into a noisy carnival world of tents and sideshows, food stands and taverns.

A throng around a gaming arena parted; the three stepped back as litter bearers hurried past with an unconscious boxer, gloves of hardened leather on his hands.

Overhead, an air-walker, a great long pole in hand, picked his way out onto a quivering stretch of rope. A contortionist walked on her hands, her legs wrapped around her back, her feet on her waist. A mime, his face painted white, walked up to Linlin and looked at her with wide eyes and a stretched smile; he pointed at her and then at himself, put his hands together prayerfully, and silently asked her to marry him.

She giggled and blushed, and made a sad face and shook her head no.

With an exaggerated pout on his face, the mime slumped away in slow motion.

A horse snorted; leading it by the reins, a constable went past. He looked at the three without interest and continued on.

"*Sheren!*" "The snake-man!" a little girl chortled, running with her friends to where a crowd was closing in a circle around a tall man.

"What does *he* do?" asked Linlin as they pressed near.

Wearing a dirty white robe, his long hair and beard hanging in greasy ringlets, the man plucked a fat, writhing snake from a basket. He stroked it and seemed to be whispering to it as it coiled around his arm. He kissed its flat head—and then held it aloft by the tail, and opening his mouth wide, swallowed the thing, whole and alive.

"Eeew!" squealed a little girl in front of Baoliu, watching through her fingers.

The man approached the crowd. He stopped, looked from face to face, and then, smiling, beat openhanded on his chest. The third time he struck himself, his chest began to heave and convulse. For a moment, he seemed to be choking. His mouth opened, and as the crowd groaned in revulsion and disbelief, the head of the snake appeared, its forked tongue flickering. More of the beast emerged as the man opened his mouth ever wider, and the whole of the thing slithered out into his waiting hands.

The performance wasn't over.

The man reached into the basket again—and pulled out a wriggling handful of small white snakes. And then one by one he began swallowing them.

"I think I've seen enough!" said Linlin, sticking her tongue out and then heading away.

Baoliu and Zhou hurried to catch up to her.

"That was so disgusting, wasn't it?" she asked as they walked.

"I sort of liked it," said Zhou, grinning mischievously.

Lin looked at Baoliu.

"Me, too." He laughed.

"You're both idiots!" She groaned, smiling in spite of herself. And then laughed out loud as a trained bear walked past, carrying a full-grown man in its shaggy arms.

Baoliu inhaled; his mouth began to water. From stands and taverns ahead wafted the delicious aroma of food.

"It's been two days since we've eaten," he said. "And we haven't got a tongqian between us," added Linlin.

"We'll find something," said Zhou, scanning the way ahead. Baoliu took hold of Linlin's wrist, following after Zhou as they wended their way through a moving maze of people.

A man gnawed on a beef bone as he walked past. A woman had a spiced plum-on-a-stick, and so did a little girl trotting behind her. Baoliu wanted to grab the food from their hands. He swallowed hard and took Linlin's hand, trying to keep up with Zhou.

"Where is he going?" asked Linlin.

"He knows what he's doing," said Baoliu as they picked their way between two food stands and then found Zhou behind a tavern, picking through garbage.

"I'd rather steal—and get something decent," said Zhou. "But it's too dangerous. This will have to get us by."

It was repulsive, but Baoliu was too hungry to care. They ate as they went, stuffing themselves with whatever they could find—orange peels, soya beans, stale rolls, bits of meat and gristle from rabbit bones—anything that looked edible.

"Here," said Linlin. On her knees, she was gathering overripe peaches and filling a broken basket with them. "There's a lot," she said, getting up and showing Baoliu and Zhou her find—and then she froze, as a Jinwo constable trotted past, gave them a long, hard look, and continued on.

"Don't worry about him," said Zhou, as the constable disappeared from view. "It's not a crime to eat garbage!"

Behind a gambling parlor, they feasted on the peaches. "Not bad!" Zhou murmured, as they finished the last of the fruit. He wiped sticky hands on his pants. "Better than what you get in prison. I'd rather eat garbage than that."

"When were you in prison?" asked Linlin.

"Until last year."

"Where?"

"Hangzhou."

"For what?"

"Stealing. My brother and I stole a blanket—a stinking *horse* blanket."

"How long were you in prison?" asked Baoliu, realizing Zhou was finishing a story he'd begun long ago.

"About eight months."

"How long have you been out?"

"Over a year."

"Your 'brother'?" said Linlin questioningly. "Who was your brother?"

"His name was Po Sin. He died the first week there."

Linlin put a hand to her mouth. "I'm so sorry," she said.

"The guards beat him—and did other things." Zhou spat. "Night after night. And then one night he didn't come back from the guardhouse. In the morning, I was given a spade and told to bury my brother."

"How old was he?" asked Baoliu, clearing his throat.

"Nine." Zhou looked at them somberly. "There were eleven in my family. All of them died in the plague. Only my brother Po Sin and I survived. And somehow we managed to get by—for five years, until we were put in prison.

"He died. He was murdered, and so was I. The rest of the time I was in that place, I was dead. The only thing I did was count the days—and fight when I had to. I didn't have any friends in prison, and none outside—not until I met . . ." He grinned at Baoliu and gave him a good-natured shove. "Not until I met this crazy fool have I really had much to do with anybody."

"The two of you—how long have you been friends?" asked Linlin.

Baoliu scratched his bristled scalp. "When was the fight with Chen Mingna?" he asked Zhou.

"Couple of months ago, maybe longer."

"You met in a fight?" asked Linlin incredulously. "How do you *meet* in a fight?"

"It isn't easy," said Baoliu, forcing a smile.

"What was the fight about?"

"A few monkey butts decided to give me a beating. Zhou stepped in and helped me out. Saved my sorry life."

"Why did they want to beat you up?"

"It's hard to explain," said Baoliu, feeling his palms suddenly start to sweat. "They thought that I was a—" he began, stumbling over his words.

"Is something wrong?"

"No."

"If you don't feel like telling me, it's all right," said Linlin. "Really."

"But I *do* want to tell you," said Baoliu, looking from Zhou to Linlin. "I have to."

"You 'have to'? What do you mean?"

Baoliu took a deep breath, and his gaze met hers. "The rich boy—the one your father died in place of. Linlin, that's me."

"WHAT?" LINLIN SAID, knitting her brow. "What are you talking about?"

"It's the truth," said Baoliu. "I'm the one your father died in place of. I'm the rich boy."

"No, it can't be," she said, exhaling the words. She looked at Zhou. "Is this a joke?"

"No," said Zhou, "it isn't."

Linlin sat back on her heels and hung her head. "I don't believe it," she said, staring down at her hands pressed against her lap. "I don't!"

"I'm so sorry," said Baoliu.

She looked up at him. "How could you do this to me?" she said, wiping at tears. "Especially you?"

"I didn't mean to hurt you, not in any way."

"It was all a lie, wasn't it? All along. And it wasn't any accident that we met, was it?"

"No," said Baoliu, shaking his head, and watching as a drunken man staggered out the back door of the gambling parlor.

"That morning, when the two of you had that frog meat—and shared it with Grandfather and me—that was all a part of getting to me, wasn't it?"

"Yes."

"And all you are is a rich boy pretending to be poor!"

"No," said Baoliu. "I'm not *pretending* at all! I'm as poor as anybody. My father disowned me."

"But you still had money?"

"No. None. And I didn't have a friend, either, not until I met Zhou. And then I met you and your grandfather, Shen Pang. And things just happened. I wanted to tell you, but I didn't know how."

"But what made you come to me in the first place?"

"I *had* to."

" 'Had to'? Why? What for?"

"I don't know. Maybe just to tell you that I'm innocent, and that I'm not just some rich brat that got away with murder." Baoliu opened his hands to her. "I was convicted of killing my father's second wife. I didn't, and I don't feel guilty about any of that. But your father—that's what bothers me. It's him—he's the one I feel like I killed."

"No, *you* didn't," said Linlin. "Your *father* did. My father worked for him—but you know that, don't you?"

"Yes."

"And what he did when my father was hurt—do you know *that* as well?"

"Yes, I'm afraid I do," said Baoliu, hanging his head.

"If only he had helped my father after he was hurt. But he didn't. He did nothing!"

"I know."

"But still, you—" began Linlin, and then paused as a sudden loud cheering from inside the gambling parlor drowned out her voice. "You say your father disowned you. Why?"

Baoliu opened his mouth to answer, and then looked up at several constables racing toward them down a slope.

"They're Jinwo constables, but they're coming for *us!*" sputtered Zhou, getting to his feet.

"The crowd—get into the crowd!" cried Linlin.

Baoliu grabbed her arm. "This way!" he yelled, and then pushed her ahead of him through the back door of the gambling parlor. And then he and Zhou were scrambling after her through the place—knocking over a mahjong table, and then stumbling through a huddled group of gamblers—cards and money flying from their hands. He saw Linlin disappear out the front entrance and then tripped over Zhou and fell sprawling with him into a dice game.

"What do you think you're doing?" snarled a man, pushing Baoliu off him.

"Idiot!" hissed another.

"Come on!" Baoliu yelled, trying to pull Zhou to his

feet. And then he let go and backed away as a half-dozen constables poured in through both doors.

"Damn!" cursed Zhou, getting to his knees and then putting his hands together in front of him. "Don't fight them," he told Baoliu as constables surrounded them.

Baoliu looked up at the point of a dagger, and extended his hands.

A constable in hardened-leather armor pushed his way into the gambling parlor, gawking patrons making way for him.

"These the ones you were looking for?" a Jinwo constable asked the one from Yongjia, his gaze on half-closed lumps of flesh where the man's nose should have been.

"Where's the girl?"

"We already have men looking for her. She went in the back of this place and out the front, into the crowd. We'll find her."

"On orders from the magistrate, she's to be . . . taken care of. And these two. . . ." He looked at Baoliu and Zhou, sitting with their hands bound—and then grinned broadly.

"You!" he hissed and grabbed Baoliu by the collar. "You remember me? You remember what I told you would happen if you was lying to me?" He huffed through the hole in his face. "Told you you'd die, didn't I?" He gloated, patting Baoliu's cheek with a leather-gloved hand. "Well, you're going to die, boy!"

Baoliu looked at Zhou, and then hung his head.

"What do you want done with them?" asked a Jinwo constable.

"These two are to be returned to Yongjia," he said, using Baoliu's head to push himself to his feet. "See to it."

13

BAOLIU AND ZHOU spent the rest of the afternoon with drunks, thieves, and brawlers in a holding cell on the edge of the Pleasure Grounds. With the coming of night, lanterns were lit, hundreds of them, creating a world of shimmering blues, pinks, and greens.

One by one, the others were released or taken to jail. Baoliu and Zhou were taken down to the harbor and put aboard a military ship and locked in the hold apart from each other, Baoliu in a tiny wooden cell, Zhou in a storage area. The ship, a supply vessel, got underway that night, arriving on the docks in Yongjia midafternoon of the following day. From there, the two were taken to Yongjia Prison.

In shackles, guards herded them into a torch-lit corridor, their arrival triggering howls of derision from the prisoners. Their fingers laced around bars, they watched Baoliu and Zhou pass, taunting and laughing at them, and cursing the guards.

"I hope you will be happy here." A guard smiled, swinging open a cell door.

Baoliu followed Zhou inside.

The door slammed behind them; a key clicked in the lock, and then footsteps headed away, drowned out by a new round of outbursts from the prisoners.

The cell was tiny, filthy, and reeked of urine. Decorated with graffiti, the walls glistened damply, and black mold grew in corners and crevices. Flies blanketed a wooden waste bucket, and overhead, rats traveled unseen through the rafters.

Baoliu pulled himself up to look out the only window in the place—and saw the main square of Yongjia, far below.

"Why did they bring us here?" he asked Zhou, dropping back to the floor. "It doesn't make any sense. They could have locked us up in Jinwo, but instead they bring us back to Yongjia. Why?"

"They want something," said Zhou.

Baoliu nodded. "Yeah, but what?"

"That, I don't know."

Baoliu gripped the barred door and looked across the corridor. From the cells across the way, a sullen gallery of faces gazed back at him. He turned to Zhou. "I'm so sorry for getting you into this."

"It's not your fault."

"Isn't it? You've stuck with me through everything. And because of it, this is where you end up."

"What about Linlin? Do you think she got away?" asked Zhou, changing the subject.

"I hope so." Baoliu picked at an itching sore between two fingers. "She's smart; she's tough."

"Smart? Yes. But not *that* tough, not as much as she pretends. And look what she's up against."

"The stinking constables. And if they find her, they'll kill her."

"And before that, they'll do worse," said Zhou.

"A beautiful girl like Linlin—who would want to hurt someone like *that*?"

"They would."

"It makes me sick to think about it." Baoliu shook his head. "I've never known anyone like her." He pursed his lips. "I just wish things had been different."

"She was in love with you."

"Maybe for a while. But not anymore. Not after what I told her."

"She doesn't blame you. She blames your father."

Baoliu shrugged. "Whatever she thinks of me, it really doesn't matter anymore, does it?" He looked around the cell. "All of that is over. All there is now is this."

"What's going to happen to us?"

"What's to become of *you*, I don't know," said Baoliu. "I hope it's nothing worse than slavery. I think that's the best you can hope for, I'm sorry to say."

"How about you?" asked Zhou.

"They'll have my head. I've already been found guilty of whatever new crimes they decide to charge me with. And because that means I violated the laws of *ka-di*, I'll be retried for a murder—one I've already been convicted of, and will be again. But for you, there's still hope." He frowned. "I only hope that luck will be with you."

"It will. And it will be with you, too," said Zhou, the smile on his face betrayed by the look in his eyes.

A SINGLE GUARD came for Baoliu that night. An older man—quiet, almost deferential—he led Baoliu from his cell and then up a spire of stairs and into a narrow vestibule. Ahead, gray light spilled from a doorway, and the aroma of incense suddenly filled the air.

"In here, please," said the guard, gesturing Baoliu ahead of him into the room.

Baoliu recoiled.

Writing at a lectern, the magistrate looked up. "Ah,

welcome," he said, an amused grin on his face. "How nice it is to see you again!"

In chains, Baoliu walked to the bearded man, looking him in the eye.

"May I offer you some refreshment? Tea, perhaps? Plum cakes?"

"No, thank you."

"No?" Lizard eyes blinked. "Then allow me to proceed with the matter at hand," he said, producing a scroll from the hidden world within the sleeves of his robe. "Allow me to proceed quickly to the heart of the matter, and not further intrude upon your undoubtedly already busy schedule." A smile twitched on his lips. "You are in violation of the accord of *ka-di*, as I would assume you are aware. The pertinent provision," he announced, and then read from the scroll: "*. . . he shall be allowed to live, until such a time as he might, through misconduct or criminal endeavor, prove himself unworthy of this clemency; and revocation of these proceedings in this matter shall be undertaken.*"

The magistrate rested his hands on the lectern. "Do you understand what I have just read?"

"Yes."

"Then you understand that you are to be retried on the charge of murdering your father's wife—that is, of course, if you are found guilty of additional charges to be brought before the court."

"What are the charges?"

"Attack upon a constable in the lawful performance of his duty; subversion; and abetting the flight of a fugitive."

"Of Shen Linlin?" asked Baoliu.

"Indeed! How quick you are!"

"What do you want from me?" asked Baoliu.

The magistrate rested his chin on a forefinger. "Your confession to all charges."

"What? Why would I confess?"

"It would make things easier for me."

"Make things easier for you?" Baoliu smiled crookedly. "And why would I want to do *that*?"

"To allow you to die with a modicum of dignity."

"What do you mean?"

"Your comrade, your accomplice, Wanlun Zhou, will face similar charges, and like you, will undoubtedly be found guilty and most likely executed. I offer you the chance to save his life. For your confession, he will be set free."

"'Set free'?" Baoliu swelled with relief. "And the charges dismissed?"

The magistrate nodded. "Unless you attempt, at any time, including at your trial, to withdraw your confession. His life would then be forfeit."

"And the girl—Shen Linlin?" he asked hopefully. "Will you grant her the same? Has she been found? Is she alive?"

"You test my patience!" hissed the magistrate, long

fingernails drumming on the table. "Your confession? Will I have it—or shall I reconsider my offer?"

Baoliu nodded. "You will have it."

WHEN BAOLIU WAS returned to the cell, it was empty, and the door ajar—and far down the corridor, lit yellow by torchlight, he could see a familiar figure being escorted from the prison.

"Zhou!" he yelled.

"Baoliu!" Zhou's voice echoed back down the corridor. "What have you done? What have you done?"

The heavy door at the end of the corridor opened. For a moment, Zhou was framed in a rectangle of light, and then he was gone.

THE PRISONER IN the cell across from Baoliu had gone insane. He had ugly lumps on his forehead, and day after day told Baoliu, and anyone who would listen, that he had seashells growing out of his head. That was his punishment, he said, for killing his wife—though it was known his wife had come to visit him.

The prisoner in the cell next to Baoliu's seemed strangely content, and endlessly hummed a private medley of songs. The two prisoners to the other side of him told Baoliu they had been captured in the peasants' revolt in Fuzhou the year before. They claimed imperial troops had killed more than ten thousand people, and had lost almost half that many of their own. They also said there would be a revolt in Yongjia soon if things did not change.

Baoliu told his own story, without mention of the *ka-di*.

Talking, scratching off the days on the wall, and hunting cockroaches—they were the only diversions. Like the others, Baoliu kept a watch for roaches—driven by hate, hunger, and the pleasure of the hunt—he pounced on them whenever they scuttled out from gaps in the walls and floor, and crushed them with his heel or hammered them with the side of his fist. And then, like the others, he mixed the pasty remains into the evening meal—the only meal of the day—a half bowl of watery rice.

Not eating the roaches, the others told Baoliu, would cause him to have sores on his skin.

Though he did as they advised, a sore had already begun to grow on an ankle, and his skin itched infernally. Cuts and scratches didn't heal. His hands and feet started looking puffy. And his bones ached from the cold and damp. He became listless. Day after day, he sat, waiting for whatever was to come, and wanting it to be over.

When he woke one morning to his door squeaking open, he thought his trial had come.

"You have a visitor," said a young-looking guard as Hai Nan stepped tentatively into the cell.

"You have five minutes," said the guard, shutting the barred door on the two of them.

"Baoliu?" In a frayed robe, Hai Nan stared down at

him. "Baoliu, is that you?" he asked, his eyes traveling the cell, a hand to his nose against the stench.

"What do you want?" asked Baoliu wearily, wondering at the tears in his brother's eyes.

"What has happened to you?" exclaimed Hai Nan, kneeling down beside him. "Are you all right? What have they done to you?"

"How did you find me?"

"Your friend—the boy Zhou—he found us. He told us what happened to you and where you were."

"Zhou? He's all right?"

"Yes. And so's the girl."

"Linlin? She's alive?" exclaimed Baoliu.

"She traveled the back roads from Jinwo, and got here three days ago. She was looking for you, and came to us. She and I—and Father—have been talking."

"She's met Father?"

"At first she was very cold to us. She thought Father had just turned his back on her father when he burned his hands. But that's not quite what happened. There was a lot she didn't know."

"And what's that?"

"Shen Manfong fought with Father about getting his job back."

"I know. I was there."

"But after Shen Manfong left, Father felt badly about the whole thing. He came up with an idea to help the man, and sent me to look for him—to offer him work running errands and cleaning up." Hai Nan frowned. "But I couldn't find him.

"Weeks later—as Father and I were closing up—he came to the shop. We thought he'd come to ask for work or money. But before Father had a chance to tell him about the job, Shen Manfong offered himself in *ka-di*. Father jumped at the chance." Hai Nan shrugged. "Linlin and Father—I think they're both starting to see everything a lot more clearly, now."

"Where is Linlin?"

"With us, and so is the boy."

"Linlin and Zhou are *staying* with you?"

"Yes, in town."

"*'In town'*?"

"We've lost the house. We only have what remains of the business, and live on the second floor, above the shop. We're trying to start over. Things have been hard—but that's not why I'm here."

"Why, then?"

"Your trial will be tomorrow."

"'Tomorrow'?" said Baoliu, parroting his brother, feeling a sudden twinge of nervous fear and picturing the courtroom in his head.

"I've been trying to see you for days, but they wouldn't allow it. And Father was unable to come. He wanted to, but didn't have the strength."

"Is something wrong with him? Is he sick?"

"Yes. He has been ever since he learned you were in

prison. But it's *you* that I came to talk about. And I have no time. Only a moment—that's all they've allowed me." He looked back through the bars at the guard.

"Did you say that Father wanted to see me? He's forgiven me?"

"It's himself he can't forgive."

"What? Why?"

"The guilt he feels."

"About what?"

"About everything that's happened to you."

"What do you mean?"

"He knows that you're innocent."

Baoliu stared.

"He knows, just like I do now, that you couldn't have been the one who robbed and killed Jia Lam."

"What do you mean, *you know*? I don't understand. What are you talking about?"

"The day that you and Zhou came to the shop—afterward, Father and I began to talk. We talked again that night, and it came to us why you couldn't have committed the crime. We told the magistrate, but he dismissed us. He simply listened to us and then told us he'd consider the matter. We've heard nothing from him since."

"*What* did you tell him?" urged Baoliu, his words obliterated by the guard rattling a club across the bars.

"Come," the guard ordered Hai Nan. "I've given you more time than I should."

"One more moment!" Hai Nan begged.

"Now!"

"Why? Why do you and Father believe I'm innocent?"

"Because of the stolen jewelry."

"What do you mean?"

"Did you not hear me?" demanded the guard, his keys rattling in the lock.

"The jewelry, it proves you're innocent."

"What? How? How does it prove anything?"

"It's complicated. But trust me. It *is* proof!"

"But it doesn't matter anymore." Baoliu shook his head. "It doesn't matter what you say in court."

"What do you mean?" asked Hai Nan, as the guard stormed into the cell.

"I've already confessed."

GUARDS CAME FOR him early the next morning. "It's time, boy," said one, opening the cell door. Another removed Baoliu's leg shackles, and then led the way, down the corridor and across the main yard. Slaves opened a massive gate of bronze, and ahead loomed the House of Law, a four-story monolith of time-darkened stone.

The *Genggu*, The Drum of Time, announced the seventh hour of the morning as Baoliu was escorted into a courtroom, one much larger than that in which he had been condemned to death three months earlier. At the bench sat the same judge—in black robes, one hand resting on an ivory cudgel as he pored over a document.

Baoliu heard someone laugh, and wondered if it was at him. He wondered at the great number of people filling the place. Most of them looked poor. He tried to spot Linlin, but could not, and wondered if she was even there. He saw his father, and then Zhou and a woman he recognized from the ravine. He looked for others he knew, for family and friends, and then recoiled at the sight of the magistrate. In robes of peacock blue, seated apart from the others, he smiled imperiously as Baoliu passed.

Absentmindedly, the judge pounded his cudgel against the floor, but didn't look up as the court fell silent and Baoliu was led to stand before him. Instead, he continued reading, thumbing through a clutter of documents spread before him.

"Tang Baoliu," he finally muttered. "On behalf of the office of the magistrate," he said, "and in accordance with imperial law, you have been charged with attacking a constable in the lawful performance of his duties, seditious conduct, and abetting the flight of a fugitive, one Shen Linlin. Do you contest these charges?"

Baoliu swallowed hard. "No, I do not," he said, a sudden uproar of protest and disbelief swelling the courtroom.

"Silence!" the judge demanded, pounding with his ivory cudgel—his gaze traveling over the audience as the din subsided.

A clerk in a red skullcap quietly placed additional documents on the table.

The judge nodded to the man and then returned his attention to Baoliu. "You acknowledge your guilt?"

Baoliu looked at the magistrate. And then looked back at his father and brother, and saw Zhou and Linlin, too.

"Do you or do you not acknowledge your guilt?" demanded the judge.

Baoliu clenched his jaw. "Yes."

"Your plea will be noted; however, information has been received by this court contradicting a verdict of guilty. Though noted, your plea is rejected; by order of the provincial governor, the charges are dismissed."

"What? Why?" Baoliu stared, his mouth agape.

"No evidence of seditious conduct has been found. As to abetting the flight of a fugitive: quite simply, one cannot do so if that person is not by law a fugitive. I speak of Shen Linlin. Since no charges had been filed against her at the time she was pursued, her conduct was not unlawful, and therefore, neither was yours. And finally, as to the charge of assault: testimony taken from those in attendance at the funerary gathering indicates that the constable exceeded his authority; his use of force was illegitimate and malicious, and he has been taken into custody."

"If he is found guilty of wrongdoing, I hope he shall be dealt with most harshly!" announced the magistrate, rising to his feet. "And so, too, should any others who may have conducted themselves improperly!"

The judge looked at him impassively, and then addressed Baoliu: "By virtue of dismissal of these charges,"

continued the judge, "there are no new bad acts on your part to warrant retrial on the charge of murder—of one Tang Jia Lam. However, in that you have confessed in writing to these charges, no new bad acts are required to proceed with retrial. By the power of these courts, your confession is hereby accepted, your former conviction noted, and I again find you guilty of this crime."

Baoliu slowly turned and looked at the magistrate, and in that moment understood what the man had done to him, and how he had been fooled by him.

"And now I know," he blurted out, "why you needed my confession! Without it, I would have been freed!"

The magistrate smiled, smoothing his blue silk robe.

"Do you wish to make a statement?" asked the judge. "Do you wish to withdraw your confession?"

"Withdraw it!" Zhou called out.

"Be silent!" the judge demanded, and then repeated his question. "Tang Baoliu, do you wish to reconsider your confession?"

He shook his head. "I cannot," he said.

"'Cannot'?" asked the judge, his gaze traveling from Baoliu to the magistrate.

"No, I do not withdraw my confession."

"Very well, then, in that your guilt has been confirmed, I now address those assembled and ask if anyone wishes to speak in defense of Tang Baoliu. Are any so inclined?"

It was his father's voice that Baoliu heard next.

"*I* am so inclined!"

Baoliu looked back, and saw his father stand, and saw how gray he had become and how old he now looked.

"My son could not have committed this crime," he said, his words loud but tremulous. "It is not possible!"

"How so?" asked the judge.

"The stolen jewelry is itself the proof."

"I fail to understand."

"Seven pieces of jewelry were stolen and never recovered. On the night of the crime, Baoliu was found unconscious in the house, outside the sleeping quarters of Jia Lam. If he never left the house, how did he manage at the same time to get away with the seven pieces of jewelry? How?"

"A fascinating point," said the judge. "Fascinating indeed!"

"May I be heard?" asked the magistrate, and then continued without awaiting a response. "There could be numerous explanations. For one, the boy may well have had an accomplice, and this person—or persons—escaped with the jewelry."

"There was *no* accomplice!" shouted Baoliu's father. "That is absurd!"

"Is it?" asked the magistrate insouciantly. "Then might I submit yet another explanation for your consideration—that the items were pilfered by persons unknown during the confusion following the murder? Is that not possible?"

Baoliu's father said nothing.

"Or perhaps the boy took these pieces prior to the night of the murder, and not until then was it discovered that they were missing." He sighed affectedly. "What became of the jewelry is of no significance. And—"

"Enough!" said the judge, interrupting him. "Your point has been made." Exhaling wearily, he looked out at the courtroom. "Are there any others who care to speak on behalf of the accused?"

"I would," said someone from the back of the room.

Baoliu turned at the sound of the familiar voice, and his heart raced as Linlin rose to her feet.

"Guards!" snarled the magistrate. "Seize that girl! She is the seditionist we have been pursuing! Seize her!"

"Let her speak!" Spectators rose to their feet and shouted—the shout becoming a chant. "Let her speak!"

"Guards! Do your duty!" ordered the magistrate.

The guards hesitated, and looked from the magistrate to the judge, unsure of what to do.

"Stand down!" thundered the judge. "She will be heard!"

"I protest!" exclaimed the magistrate.

"Ni jiang guo duole!" "Enough from you!" snapped the judge, pointing his cudgel at the magistrate. "Your authority does not extend to the House of Law!"

"Linlin," Baoliu murmured under his breath as she approached the judge.

"Who are you, young lady?" asked the judge.

"I am Shen Linlin, the daughter of Shen Manfong, who was executed in *ka-di*, in place of Baoliu."

"And you wish to speak on *his* behalf?"

"Yes."

"In defense of one whose life continued at the cost of your own father's?"

"I do."

"And what is it you wish to say?"

"That Tang Baoliu is innocent—that he did not kill the woman."

"And why do you believe this?"

"Because I know who did."

The judge laced his fingers together. "And who is that?"

Linlin hesitated.

"Who killed her?"

"My father."

"YOUR FATHER MURDERED Jia Lam?" the judge exclaimed, his words muted by an excited drone from the crowd. He pounded for quiet, and as the babble subsided, repeated the question.

"My father was employed by the father of Tang Baoliu for more than twenty years. When he was crippled while working, Baoliu's father—or so we believed—turned his back on us. We ran out of money and then out of food, and there was no work of any kind. We were starving.

We had nothing—while his employer had far more than he needed.

"One night my father slipped away without telling anyone; when he returned, just before sunrise, he was covered in blood, and then he showed us—my grandfather and me—the jewelry. And he wept as he told us what he'd done, that he'd killed someone, a woman."

"Jia Lam?" asked the judge.

"Yes."

"Please, go on."

"He didn't mean to. He startled her from her sleep, and when she tried to scream he put his hand over her mouth. There were sewing shears. She tried to stab him with them, and when he grabbed her arm, the shears hit her in the throat.

"When my father learned that Baoliu, his employer's son, was to be executed for the crime, he was distraught. He said that he was going to confess. But then he thought of *ka-di*—a way to save the boy, and to save his family, at the same time."

"What became of the jewelry?" asked the judge.

"Before offering himself in *ka-di*, my father used it to buy a potter's shop—for me, my grandfather, and for the rest of the family. The magistrate found out about the purchase, and that the jewelry bore the design of the house of Tang Qin. He realized it was the stolen jewelry."

"The magistrate knew this *before* the accord?" asked the judge.

"Yes."

"Who has the jewelry now?"

"The magistrate. He confiscated it."

" 'Confiscated it'?" asked the judge. He looked at the magistrate, jotted down a note, and then returned his attention to Linlin.

"The shop you purchased—what became of it?"

"It was also confiscated by the magistrate."

"What did you do with the money from the *ka-di*?"

"We never received any of it."

"Why?"

"The magistrate threatened to reveal what my father had done, and that he was, as he said, a thief and a murderer, not the hero that others believed him to be. He said it would be at the cost of my father's reputation that I would be paid the two thousand."

" 'Two thousand'?" asked the judge, writing as he spoke. "What do you mean?"

"The two thousand we had been promised for the *ka-di*."

"You were to have been paid *four* thousand, not two," he said, and then looked at the magistrate. "Or am I mistaken?"

"I will have the matter looked into," he said fawningly. "Perhaps there was a mistake, a misunderstanding."

"Go on," the judge told Linlin.

"When the magistrate threatened to expose my father, I threatened to expose the magistrate—not just for what he did to me, but for what he does to everybody. I told him I was going to go to his superiors. When I said that, he sent constables—"

"I will hear no more of this!" The magistrate rose. "I must—"

"Be seated," said the judge. "*That* is what you must do."

He sat, and crossed his arms as a child might do, and glowered, petulantly.

Linlin aimed a finger at him. "What the magistrate has done to my family is only one small instance of what he does to the people of Yongjia every day. He is, to my mind, the most dangerous criminal in the city."

"I protest this vicious slander!" yelled the magistrate, again on his feet.

"I think you waste your time protesting to me," said the judge. And then he smiled. "Instead, I believe you will be protesting your innocence to the judiciary in Hangzhou."

"How dare you threaten me?"

"Guards," ordered the judge, "take the magistrate into custody."

Howls of outrage were drowned out by howls of laughter as a peacock-blue figure ran—then slapped and kicked as a guard grabbed him. "I am the magistrate!" he squealed. And started to announce himself again as another guard shoved a leather gag into his mouth.

"Remove him," said the judge, and then he watched

as the magistrate was dragged kicking and writhing from the courtroom.

The spectators cheered.

The judge turned to Linlin. "There is still one thing I do not understand," he said. "You hold your father's name and reputation in high regard. And yet you risked sullying his name for the sake of Tang Baoliu? Why?"

"To save one who is innocent, and one whom I have come to know and to admire."

"Or perhaps you have concocted a story—simply trying to save someone you have come to care for? Moreover, despite your testimony, considerable evidence of Tang Baoliu's guilt was presented at the first trial and must be restudied. Finally, there is a significant amount of money involved here, and how it has affected both your declaration and that of Tang Qin must also be taken into consideration."

The judge looked at Linlin and Baoliu and then out at the gallery. "There will be a short recess before I render my verdict."

BAOLIU WAS TAKEN to the guards' changing room and told to sit in a corner on a stack of sleeping mats. A young guard, a heavyset boy not much older than Baoliu, locked Baoliu's wrist and ankle chains together.

"Could you do me a favor?" asked Baoliu, as the

guard finished up. "Could you give someone a message for me?"

"Sure. No problem," said the guard.

"Thank you," said Baoliu.

"Who's the message for and what do you want me to say?"

"My father. He's the gray-haired man who spoke for me."

"I remember him."

"Tell him that *Mother's things are in the cypress tree*," said Baoliu, and then repeated the message. "He'll understand," he said, and looked up as his father and brother stepped into the room.

"It seems you can tell him yourself," said the guard, getting up and stepping aside.

Baoliu looked up at his father, not sure of where to begin. "The things I took long ago, after Mother died, are in a crevice in the largest of the cypress trees," he said.

"Thank you, Baoliu. But they are *your* things now. I want you to have them—as soon as the trial is over." He smiled nervously, unconvincingly. "You'll see. You will be cleared!"

"I wish I were as sure as you are," said Baoliu. He smiled wistfully. "I don't know what the judge will say. I only know how much it meant to me that you stood up for me in court."

"I should have stood up for you before!"

"But I know why you didn't, Father. All the evidence

pointed at me, and with the way I'd been treating you—
and Jia Lam. . . . I had no right to judge you, or her—or
to behave like I did. I know that now."

"Still, I should have stood by you!"

"You did. You saved my life—at a terrible cost to you.
Your business—I'm so sorry about what has happened
to it. I know what it means to you."

"I don't care about the business! I only care about—"
Tang Qin stopped himself and hung his head.

"Baoliu," said Hai Nan, putting an arm around their
father. "Why did you confess? Why?"

"Because I let the magistrate play me for a fool. He
told me that confessing was the only way to save Zhou."

"You confessed to save your friend?"

"Please, you can't ever tell him!"

Hai Nan nodded slowly, his gaze meeting his brother's.

"No matter what," said Tang Qin, his lips trembling,
"I am proud of you, son."

Baoliu looked up through tears in his eyes—and saw
a scribe hurrying into the room. "The judge has reached
a decision," he announced.

THE COURTROOM WAS silent when Baoliu returned.
With Linlin next to him, he stood before the judge.

For a long moment, the dark-robed man studied a
document, and then looked up. "Shen Linlin," he said.

She stiffened.

"It is the decision of this court that the money promised by the accord of *ka-di* was illegally withheld from you. It shall be paid in full, and with the court's sincere apology."

Baoliu touched Linlin's arm. "Good!" he whispered.

She smiled halfheartedly, her brow furrowed with worry, her eyes on his.

"Moreover," continued the judge, "the money shall be paid by the office of the magistrate and not, as originally stipulated, by Tang Qin, father of Tang Baoliu. The sum of eight thousand tongqian is deemed to have been taken from Tang Qin by fraudulent means; that is, pertinent information was being withheld from him at the time he signed the accord of *ka-di*. The money shall be returned to him forthwith."

Baoliu looked back at his father—and saw that his head was bent, as though waiting for news of more importance.

"Tang Baoliu," said the judge.

Baoliu took a deep breath.

"It is the decision of this court, on behest of the divine Ninzong, that the verdict of this court be reversed and that you be declared innocent of any crime. The disgrace you once bore in error, you also bore with dignity; you have honored yourself and your family. You may go, and may the fates treat you kindly. I wish you luck."

"*Huzzah!*" shouted Hai Nan.

"*Huzzah!*" shouted the others in resounding agreement.

Baoliu bowed to them—and hung his head, and wept.

He felt a hand on his shoulder, and looked at Linlin.

"Baoliu!" she cried, as their arms went around each other.

Hai Nan pushed his way out from the smiling congregation; and then his father, tears in his eyes and a great smile on his face, was there, trying to say something over the noise in the courtroom.

Zhou grabbed Baoliu's hand, and together they raised their fists.

"*Huzzah!*" roared the crowd.

ACKNOWLEDGMENTS

The author wishes to express his gratitude to Pauline Chen for her invaluable suggestions and contributions pertaining to Chinese culture, history, and language; to Dan Davis for his expert knowledge of ancient Chinese history and customs; and to his wife, Pam, for her tireless support and research during the writing of this book.